By
Eve Langlais

(Kodiak Point, Book #2)

Copyright and Disclaimer

Copyright © July 2014, Eve Langlais
Cover Art by Aubrey Rose © July 2014
Edited by Devin Govaere
Copy Edited by Amanda L. Pederick
Produced in Canada

Published by Eve Langlais
1606 Main Street, PO Box 151
Stittsville, Ontario, Canada, K2S1A3
http://www.EveLanglais.com

ISBN-13: 978-1500681029
ISBN-10: 1500681024

Chapter One

There were times when a lady had to use strong language. Unladylike language. Times such as when someone blew the tire out on a girl's awesome SUV and sent it careening off a steep embankment in the Alaskan wilds in the middle of the night. To add icing to that cake—the triple layered, buttercream frosted kind because the situation called for it—her uncontrollable descent had her skidding at a ridiculous speed toward a tree, a tree she was pretty sure wasn't going to move. So was it any wonder Jan needed to vent a little?

"Fuck!" Okay, so it wasn't a stream of invectives, but shouted at the top of her lungs, and the word stretched out, it was stronger language than Jan preferred to indulge in. Just one of her odd quirks, which tied in to her strong memories of soap and a momma who thought the best way to curb a dirty mouth was to wash it. Her dear mother didn't have any tolerance for cussing, even the most banal kind. Jan quickly learned to not repeat the naughty words the boys at school taught her, and the habit followed her into adulthood.

But facing injury or possible death, a lady could give herself a little bit of slack, especially since, "Uh-oh" and "Oh dear" just wouldn't cut it. Not when the truck—*my beautiful, almost-paid-for SUV*—hit the tree and the screeching of metal twisting, the crunch of fiberglass crushing, and the crack of glass spider-webbing all meant she'd have to go car shopping again.

While she was at it, she might need a plastic surgeon to get her nose re-adjusted. Goodness, but when that airbag deployed, it did so with speed and gusto. Sure, the inflatable bladder lessened the impact, but it hadn't stopped her from squashing her face, much like a bug on her windshield in the height of summer.

Splat.

The hard knock disoriented her, and despite her shifter ability to absorb more damage and pain than a regular human, even she had to admit she was a tad dazed and shaken up, which was why it took her a moment to realize she had company.

And not the invited kind.

A single sniff was all she needed to know the bodies trudging through the snow toward her, their blocky frames illuminated by the headlights on their snowmobiles, were shifters. Judging by the rifle slung over the shoulder of one, she doubted they were the friendly type and she was fairly positive they were idiots seeing as how they went after the unconscious and not very dangerous human who rode shotgun in her truck. *My poor pulverized truck.* A truck these guys broke.

It took a lot for Jan to lose her temper. People often commended her on her cool composure—a façade she'd practiced often because of a certain bullheaded moose who refused to admit he belonged to her. *I will trap you yet, Boris!*

However, lose her temper she did because *they broke my SUV!* And cracked a few of her freshly manicured nails, but that she could have handled.

As they wrenched the driver side door open, more like ripped it off its hinges given its warped shape, she didn't pause to think. She fired the gun she always kept close by—a present from her dear daddy. She hit her mark in the shoulder and spun him away. He apparently had no qualms about using some very vehement cuss words, which, if momma were here, would have resulted in him foaming at the mouth.

Given she was a crack shot, folks might wonder why she didn't kill him. For one thing, on the off chance she was wrong about their intent, she should probably hold off on deadly force, and second, her daddy always said, in times of war, you should always keep one of the enemy alive for questioning.

Some might argue there was no war, just a lot of jostling for power between some unknown assailant and the alpha of her clan. Jan would disagree. By attacking her poor defenseless SUV, someone had definitely thrown down a glove. Jan was more than ready to pick it up and slap them with it.

Just because she was a lady didn't mean she didn't know how to get even, or how to defend herself. Daddy made sure of that.

Using the colorful screams and curses of her downed victim as distraction, she threw herself out of her seat and hit the ground in a tucked ball, rolling to the side and popping up on one knee, gun raised.

One. Two. Three armed bad guys. Goodness, but it seemed someone had gone all out when it came to attacking her and her human passenger. Jan would have preened if she was a stupid bird. Vain creatures. Thankfully, they mostly stayed down south in the warmer climates.

"Give yourself up, fox," said a stranger who bore the unmistakable scent of caribou. A rare shifter for these parts—but tasty in a stew. "Don't make this harder than it has to be."

Did he seriously expect Jan to raise her hands and surrender? The first rule of survival, no matter your species? Never give up. Her daddy's sub-clause to it was, *and make sure you take as many down with you as you can.*

With a cheery, "Not today, boys," Jan fired in rapid succession. This time, she didn't aim to maim.

Head shot. Hit. Second, missed by a hair. A third missile went wide as something jostled her from behind.

Fetid breath washed over her. Ew. The attacking men were also using wild wolves to help them which sucked. No reasoning with those untamed creatures. And they were chomp-happy, dirty creatures.

The one who ruined her aim latched onto her wrist, only the thick layer of her jacket prevented it from breaking skin. However, given it forced her to tussle before it did some actual damage, she lost her hold on her pistol.

"My daddy gave me that gun," she complained. While irritated at the loss, she now had both her hands free which enabled her to better fight.

Tucking her legs under the writhing body of the wild wolf, she sent it flying right into an approaching assailant. Bullseye. The both went tumbling. She didn't waste the opportunity this presented.

With her gun who knew where, numbers against her, and self-preservation screaming to get her butt moving, Jan did the only thing she could. She shrugged off her coat, loosened her pants and then shifted into her other shape, twisting free of the remaining garments.

Once upon a time, she'd pondered how her adult size could compact into her much smaller arctic fox shape. She never did find a satisfactory answer but thanked the fact she had the ability as she could use her nimble and petite frame to bolt through a gap between encroaching bodies.

Beyond the initial ring of men, snowmobiles were parked haphazardly, their lights bright beacons in the dark, crisscrossing and partially blinding her. What she could see didn't bode well.

An unconscious Tammy was slung over the back of a snowmobile. Scruffy men, more than the few she'd initially counted, turned almost as one to face her and a wild pack of lean gray wolves snarled at her and ululated a battle cry.

Time to move her conditioned—and once a month hot-oil treated—white fur out of here. It galled her to have to leave Tammy in the clutches of those miscreants. But she also recognized she wouldn't do her friend any favors if she got caught in the same trap. At least if Jan remained free, she could perhaps find help.

As creatures went, Jan's vixen wasn't the largest. Nor the strongest. Nor even the most vicious. However, when it came to speed, agility, and a knack for slipping traps, her arctic fox heritage came in handy. Her snowy fur blended well with the icy landscape. In the dark, despite a shifter's enhanced eyesight, once she darted off, tracking her proved difficult. She gave a mental laugh as the curses mounted.

"Where'd the bitch go?"

How rude. I'm a vixen not a dog.

"I can't fucking see her."

Of course not. My fur is meant to blend in.

"Holy shit, I can't believe she killed Brian."

She would have killed more if given a few more minutes. She blamed her dazed state from the crash for not getting off more rounds before the wild wolf attacked. She could practically hear her daddy barking, *"Don't give me no excuses, Janny-baby. The enemy's not going to care if you're tired or on your fucking period. You have to be tougher."*

It was only because of the intervention of her mother she managed to not become the son her daddy always wanted. But she was the only girl she knew who carried a gun alongside her makeup kit in her purse.

A gun she had to leave behind during her escape. Another thing they'd pay for. Her daddy gave her that gun on her sixteenth birthday, engraved with the loving words, *Shoot to kill, Janny-baby.* Just another reason for her to hate these thugs she was escaping.

But the men after her weren't about to let her slip their grasp so easily. On the contrary, her act of defiance—and perhaps the fact she'd shot a few of them—made those remaining a tad rambunctious and determined.

Judging by the various yells behind her, she'd better tuck tail and run as fast as her four furry feet could go. At least until she came up with a better plan.

Not familiar with this part of the untamed wilds, Jan didn't know which direction to head in, nor could she stop to orient herself. She let instinct guide her. Bounding initially along packed snowmobile trails in the snow, she quickly realized she'd have to leave their relatively smooth surface if she wanted to shake her pursuers.

Off the path, she veered, weaving through the thin forest, her breath a steamy, panting fog. She just needed to put a little distance between her and her pursuers, enough that she could lay a trap.

A deadly one, just like daddy taught her.

Chapter Two

When Reid called Boris to let him know Jan was missing, along with a visiting human, the stutter of his heart had nothing to do with the vexing vixen. What did he care if the attractive receptionist—who'd made her interest clear in him since his return from the war despite his rebuffs—was missing?

This didn't stop him from snapping, "Where was she last seen?"

"Heading out of town last night."

Right into danger. Boris held in a sigh. What were the chances Jan made it from their town to the city unchallenged? Unlikely, and it would explain why the clan's attempt to net some varmints intent on causing problems had failed. His alpha, Reid, had wondered if the guy determined to challenge his leadership position had suddenly decided to behave. Given the snow fox's disappearance, along with a certain woman Reid had taken a shine to, Boris would guess he hadn't. *It seems Miss Prim and Proper Jan has bitten off more than she can chew.*

Kind of like me. He'd known for years the vixen wanted a piece of him. She made her intention quite clear. But Boris resisted. Pesky as she might be—beautiful, intelligent, and sexy beyond belief, too—Jan deserved better than an ornery bastard like him. Needed a man who didn't wake in the night with fucking nightmares, pointing his gun at a phantom enemy and clicking on empty chambers.

He'd learned after a few incidents to not sleep with a loaded weapon. Plasterwork sucked, as did waking in a rain of falling debris and dust.

But his mating situation with a certain ravishing blonde wasn't at issue here. A missing Jan was. Any member of the clan could have and would have searched for her, everyone in town loved Jan, but what did Boris do?

"I'll take my truck and go looking for her." Yeah, like a dumb fucking moose, he volunteered. He tried to justify it with the knowledge that if she was in trouble then he was best equipped to handle it. Truth was, he didn't trust anyone else to do it right. Despite his avoidance issues, Boris felt responsible for the woman. He just wouldn't sleep with or claim her like she wanted. No matter what his cock—or his moose—thought.

"Not alone you won't. We don't know what you might run into," Reid said.

"Nothing my stash can't handle." And by stash, Boris meant the mini arsenal he kept stocked in his truck. A man never knew when he might have to end or start a minor war. Or just want to shoot things for fun—and stress relief. *Stress relief that is needed every time I run into that blonde vixen and her bloody smile.*

Given he refused to hook up with her, it irritated him to no end that his body refused to honor his decision. His damned dick just couldn't stay asleep when the woman was around. And not for lack of trying!

He'd threatened it. Smacked it. Taken cold showers. And, yes, beaten it—coming with Jan's name on the tip of his tongue. Nothing ever took the edge off, not even the rare visits into the city where bars always had someone for a bastard like him. Travis called it the asshole effect; the more Boris acted aloof and uninterested, the more the ladies wanted him.

Whatever the reason for his ease in finding a temporary bedmate, Boris didn't indulge often. The sex, while okay, never filled the void in him, and the odd guilt he felt, the reason which he couldn't pinpoint, left him feeling dirty. Dirtier than a week spent in the wild without bathing. Not by choice but because he lost a fucking bet.

Boris tuned back in to Reid as he said, "I want you to take Travis with you."

"Like fuck."

"I'm making it an order."

"But he's an idiot." A young grizzly who tended to act before thinking. Boris would rather hack his own leg off than get saddled with him.

"I won't deny that, but he's got a sharp sense of smell, he's not half bad in a fight, and—"

"You want him out of your fur."

"Exactly," Reid replied, not at all chagrined in admitting the truth.

"I don't like you."

"You don't like anyone."

True. Boris grunted.

Reid laughed. "Admit it, Travis is growing on you."

"So do blood-sucking leeches. It doesn't mean I don't want to carve them off and toss them in a fire pit."

"We all want to do that with my dear cousin, but then you'd have to deal with his mother."

Boris didn't need to see Reid's shudder, not when he experienced one of his own. Everyone feared Travis' mother. "Fine. He lives. For now. Tell him to get his ass here in the next ten minutes though, or I'm leaving him behind."

Speed was of essence when it came to finding missing people, especially out here and in the winter. Shifters might prove more adaptable to the harsh climate, but predators abounded, both wild and cognitive. Bullets were also unforgiving, and Boris couldn't help but recall the thriving market for lush arctic fox fur.

No one has a nicer coat than Jan. Soft fur, pure and unblemished just like her skin, which covered a—

The fist that connected with his wall barely dented the solid wood surface. Given the plaster incidents over the years, Boris had gradually converted his interior to a more durable material. Because, again, he hated fixing drywall.

Supplies gathered, truck fueled, and with an extra gas tank strapped in the bed behind the cab, Boris sat at the wheel about to pull out when the passenger door opened and Travis hopped in.

Damn. I almost managed to escape.

"Boris, my man, I hear we're going fox and human hunting."

"Yes."

"Excellent. Two tough dudes on a quest to save the hot chicks. Do you think we'll find them?"

Boris snorted. *Of course they would. Failure was never an option.*

"I wonder if that guy who's been fucking with the clan attacked them?"

If he had, Boris would have a bone to pick with the bastard.

"Think the girls are ok—Gurg. Blerg"

Enough with the questions! Was it necessary for Boris to strangle Travis to get him to shut up? Probably not, but he did enjoy it. But thoughts of Aunt Betty-Sue—real aunt or not, no one dared call her anything else—had him ease his grip before the boy completely passed out.

Casting a wounded look his way, Travis complained. "Dude, that was so uncalled for. You know I can't fight back. You're a veteran, and my mother taught me to respect my elders."

Elder? Boris growled. "I just turned thirty-one." Which was only about six years older than the pup beside him. Some days it felt like a hundred years.

"Middle-aged, I know, and still single. That's gotta suck. Maybe if you grew a moose-tache you'd snag yourself a lady." Travis slapped his leg and laughed.

Boris gave his steering a sharp jerk and sent his passenger's head rapping off the glass. As if the young grizzly took offense. Travis chuckled harder. "You military types with your fetish for being clean shaven. Which I guess is cool. Chicks probably dig that too. On the bright side, at least you're not living in your mom's basement or something. Because that, you know, would be really pathetic."

"Says the boy still living at home."

"Hey, I'm the man of the house. I have my own bedroom upstairs, and I'm barely on my Xbox these days."

"Only because every time you logged on I kicked your ass at *Call of Duty*." A man trying to forget the war playing a war game? Don't judge him. He found it soothing—and liked following Travis' avatar around and shooting him; anger therapy that didn't leave bruises.

"One of these days, dude, we are going to have to go head to head in a Kinects Sports battle."

"Bring it, cub."

"You got it, old man."

The banal banter served its purpose. It kept Boris's mind from veering down dark paths. Twisted violent ones where he couldn't help but imagine finding Jan in a pool of blood, her lovely blue eyes staring unseeing and crimson matting her golden hair.

A vision made more concrete once he found the wreckage. He almost didn't spot it, the wind having smoothed over the tracks her SUV made when it plowed over the steep edge of the gorge. It was Travis, damn him, who spotted the clue.

"Dude, something took out the snowbank."

Which just went to show how frazzled Boris was. He should have seen it first. Usually he would have, and it was stupid little things like this that made him more determined than ever to stay away from Jan. The woman addled his mind, whether present or not.

Boris slammed on the brakes, and the truck fishtailed slightly. He hopped out of the cab and circled around to the other side for a closer look.

As if he could see much in the dark. Enhanced eyesight was all well and good, but it only went so far.

"Light," he ordered.

Travis fumbled in the back of his truck for a moment before a blinding beam lit the slope angling away from the road. Despite the wind doing its best to sweep the area clean, evidence of something plowing a trail was clear, but even more telling was the crumpled truck at the bottom of the steep embankment, its front end embracing a tree.

Boris didn't recall moving. All he knew was he half slid, half jogged down the steep incline, eyes trained on the wreck, inhaling as well as he could the scents in the area. Nothing fresh jumped out at him, but the lingering aroma of blood and animal, many animals, permeated the area. He also couldn't help but note the numerous snowmobile tracks.

Reaching the bottom, he slowed his steps as his old friend fear—a fucking asshole he kept trying to ditch but who kept coming back—made him dread peeking through the smashed driver side window of the all-too-familiar crushed SUV.

He offered up his first silent prayer in years. *Please let her be alive.* Jan might vex him, but Jan was too beautiful and bright to die so young.

A noisy breath escaped him when he saw the empty cab. No bodies. Yet.

He turned to survey the area, the shadows mocking him in the bobbing beam of the flashlight Travis brought with him.

The grizzly skidded to a stop beside him. "No sign of Jan or Tammy?"

Boris shook his head.

"Think whoever was on these sleds took her and the human chick?"

If they had, Boris would get them back.

Despite Boris' dislike of the cub, Travis was a decent tracker. Between the two of them, they pieced together events and were able to present them to Reid when he arrived.

In a nutshell, the human female got carted off, dead or alive, no one could ascertain, but Reid would go after her with a clan posse to fetch her back. It seemed his alpha, a once respectable Kodiak, had fallen for a human. Ugh. But at least this Tammy broad wasn't completely useless. The way Boris heard it, she'd faced down Reid in his Kodiak form armed with only a frying pan. That took guts, and Boris respected that.

As for Jan, she also showed more courage than he would have expected. It looked like his vixen fought back, or so he judged by the residual scent of gunpowder and trails of blood. He'd heard rumors of the fox learning to shoot with her dad. He'd not put much stock in them. Women like Jan, always perfectly coiffed and dressed, weren't the type to get their hands dirty.

Bypassing the muddle of prints and scents around the crash site, he moved outwards. While the prints were faint, he managed to locate some fox tracks leading away from the chaos. But more worrisome were the two larger sets of wolf prints and the single set of cougar ones chasing after.

Delicate Jan wouldn't stand a chance against three large predators. He only hoped she would have the common sense to run and hide. *I'm coming to get you. And if they've harmed a single hair on your head, they'll pay.*

"Want me to change into my bear to sniff out their trail?" Travis offered.

"No."

"Grab a rifle and scout?"

Boris leveled a look at him. "No."

"Guard your rear?"

"No." Boris stared at him until Travis fidgeted.

"Then what do you expect me to do?"

"Help your cousin." Yeah, he paid back his alpha by sending the cub on a new task, but truthfully, he'd fare better alone. And Reid could use the help.

While Reid's crew prepared to rev off to the rescue of the human, Boris equipped himself from the back of his truck. He could have adopted his moose form and chased after her; however, if Jan was injured or suffering from the elements, then she'd need more than just his naked body to keep her alive.

Bet her naked body could keep me alive.

Bad thought. Bad. Bad. Bad.

Checking and cataloguing his gear helped distract him from the inappropriate thoughts— backpack with bedroll, clothing, rations, light, satellite phone. On his feet, he strapped on snow shoes, the only way to truly travel where the fluffy stuff piled high, ready to suck unsuspecting trespassers into its icy jaws.

Reid shouted, "Good luck," as Boris adjusted his straps.

Boris grunted. It wasn't luck he needed but patience because when he found the disobedient fox, he'd tan her hide until she couldn't sit for a week. She'd known of the danger stalking clan members. How dare she put herself in harm's way? *Fool woman should learn to stay out of trouble.* She needed a man to keep her in line.

Me.

No, not him. But who?

Yeah, who's crazy enough to touch my fox and die?

Sigh. For a man with no interest in her, he really needed to do better when it came to jealousy issues.

Adopting a lumbering stride, the snowshoes requiring more of a lift in order to keep him upright when he ran, Boris followed the tracks. They meandered in and out of the woods. Sometimes he lost them for a stretch as Jan's fox form nimbly vaulted from exposed rock tips that jutted from the ground. But when that happened, he just had to locate the wolf marks in the snow to regain her trail.

The first body took him by surprise. The wolf, who'd obviously died too quickly to make the change back to man, stared sightlessly, his neck torn at the jugular, causing a massive and quick bleed out that few could hope to survive, although Boris knew a guy in the war who had. Tough fucker.

What he found harder to credit was all the signs pointed to Jan doing it. Ladylike, prim and proper Jan?

Jan who supposedly likes guns.

Or so he'd heard. He found it hard to believe. The Jan he knew and had first met when he accompanied Reid on a military leave had him meeting a demure young lady who inspired a man to wash his hands, hold open doors, and use the words please and thank you. That kind of femininity did not shoot guns for sport or tear out jugulars.

But still … he eyed the corpse. *Lucky bite?* Had to be. Sweet delicate Jan wasn't a killer.

He moved on, following the lupine and cougar prints chasing after the smaller vixen ones. Morning darkness eased into the few hours of daylight Alaska got this time of the year. The sunlight didn't make anything much warmer, but it did illuminate the landscape, sometimes too much at times as the sun refracted off the snow.

Tinted goggles solved that problem, but they didn't help him when he hit a rocky ridge, the fluffy snow having a hard time clinging to the solid stone surfaces. Here, at the foot, he found the second body. Also dead. A shifter in his naked man shape, a male who'd morphed in his last moments.

Boris gazed to the top of the ridge and shook his head. If he didn't know better, he'd say the dead bugger was pushed. He might have said slipped, but slipped would have placed the corpse closer to the edge of the promontory. However, the ignoble splay and face-first plant seemed to indicate foul play.

By Jan? Desperation for survival could make even the nicest person do murderous things.

Removing his snow shoes, Boris attached them to his knapsack and climbed, his heavy-duty gloves protecting his hands from the sharp edges of the rocks, but making his grip hard to maintain.

At the top, he found himself able to see for a fair distance. Nothing jumped out at him. No movement, no tracks, the top of the ridge windswept, at least the parts that were somewhat flat. Who knew what hid behind the rock boulders and humps?

Without a scent or tracks, Boris paused to take stock. Jan, the fox, was proving more resilient and wily than he would have credited. He took out a flask for a gulp of vitamin-infused liquid. He pondered his next move. Which direction would she have gone in?

"Dammit, Jan, where are you?" he muttered aloud.

"Right here," she announced before pouncing on him.

Chapter Three

Okay, so Jan should have known better than to scare a man who'd served in the military. As soon as she hit his back, legs wrapping around Boris' waist and arms around his neck, his body moved.

Boris clamped a hand around her forearm and yanked, flipping her over his head. She slammed onto her back in the snow, thankfully not atop jagged rock. But she shouldn't celebrate yet.

Still reacting to her playful attack, Boris leaped atop her, pinned her to the ground, and pointed a gun at her head. At least he didn't shoot her.

But boy, did he look annoyed.

"Hello, Boris," she said with a bright smile. "Fancy meeting you out here."

"What is wrong with you?" he yelled.

"Did I scare you?" she asked, not at all perturbed by the situation because, really, despite the violence of the act, this was the closest she'd gotten to Boris in years. And hey, he was actually looking at her. Not a point above her head. Or at the floor. Of course, his expression wasn't exactly filled with happiness, but she considered it a start.

"Are you okay?" How grudgingly he asked.

She arched a brow. "Depends. If you mean am I hurt, then no, not really. Just a few bruises and scratches. But, as for frostbite...

While I've been wanting to have you lie atop me for years, Boris Sobolev, I'd prefer a bed to a snowbank."

He growled, which, considering he was a moose, made it pretty special. As usual, she drew the most ornery of responses out of the man and had for years, especially since he returned from the war. Unfortunately, for him, she no longer cared. She'd accepted the fact Boris would never admit they were fated mates, but it didn't mean she didn't enjoy needling him every chance she got.

"You are the most irritating—"

"—ly beautiful."

"Annoying—"

"Yet utterly captivating," she interrupted with a grin.

"Woman I've ever known," he grumbled as he rolled off her to his feet. He held out a hand to help her up. Jan ignored it and lay there sprawled, naked and, yes, shivering, but the moment of frigid teeth chattering was worth it. Boris couldn't help but stare at her.

Really stare. As in eyes-devouring, body-stiffening, definitely-noticing-she-was-a-woman stare.

It did more to warm her than a pair of cashmere socks would. Although, given he wouldn't act upon the smoldering interest he forgot to hide, the socks would do her more good in the long run.

The moose took the term bullheaded to all new levels. From the moment she'd first met him, when Reid brought his new army buddy home on leave from the military, she'd known he was the one for her, and she'd thought he recognized it too.

During that short holiday stint, Boris flirted with her, and they even shared one long, delicious kiss goodbye as they exchanged a few whispered promises. But the man she dreamed of claiming was gone the next time he returned. Oh, he came back to Kodiak Point intact, no missing body parts even if he sported a few new scars, but the wounds in his soul had changed him.

Jan didn't know the exact details, but she'd heard the rumors. Reid and others in his platoon, Boris included, got caught by insurgents. More than caught, they were held captive for months and, if the gossip was true, suffered torture.

Whatever happened, the boys who'd left with smiles and boasts of kicking rebel butt returned changed men. Grimmer men. The Boris she'd fallen for, the one who made her heart race faster, who ignited all her senses, lost his easy smile. Refused to acknowledge her, and when she confronted him and asked him about murmured promises spoken before he'd left?

"Things have changed. I've changed. You need to move on and fix your sights on someone else." Bluntly honest. She could respect that, she just wished she could accept it.

But she didn't want anyone else. Although she'd tried. No other man, human or shifter, ever made her pulse quicken, her blood warm, and, with a single kiss, make her just about cream her panties. *Boris is my mate.* Even if he denied it.

Lying splayed in the snow, wanton and naked, Jan couldn't help but prolong the moment.

When else would she get a chance to see this side of Boris, his eyes smoldering with fire, his need in plain sight? For a foolish moment, she harbored the hope he'd finally admit his feelings for her. Or act upon the arousal she could see. If only she could get him to kiss her, touch her, then maybe he'd—

"If you're done trying to give your girly parts frost bite, you should think about getting dressed." He turned away from her as he dropped his loaded backpack on the snowy ground. "I've got some spare clothes in here."

Clothes? Only Boris would ignore her clear invitation and focus on the practical.

Well, Jan could be practical too. "What about a gun?"

He tossed her a look over his shoulder. "What the hell do you need a gun for?"

"To protect myself of course. There's still at least one cougar out there hunting for me. I'd like something more than just my bare hands to fight him off with."

"You've got me."

Such a chauvinistic response. She rolled her eyes. "And what if he's not alone?"

The cocky smile on anyone else would have made her laugh, but on Boris? She shivered. Even at his most menacing, the man oozed sexy.

"You are such a moose," she exclaimed under her breath as she dressed in the clothes he'd brought, not hers but small enough to fit, except for the boots. Those required three layers of socks to stay on her tiny feet.

With the chill cut, her body covered, and her prospects for getting ravished nipped in the bud, Jan focused on the situation at hand. "What's the plan?"

Without looking at her, Boris said, "We should either head back to where I left my truck. Or call in for someone to pick us up on sleds."

He called that a plan? "What about the cougar who was trailing me? He's still around here somewhere I'd wager."

"What about him?"

"Shouldn't we set a trap? Maybe take him in for questioning."

Boris turned to face her, and his tone was mocking as he said, "We? We won't be doing anything except getting your little ass back to town where it's safe."

"Safe? We're under attack. Nowhere is truly safe."

"Correction, Reid is under attack. You would have been perfectly fine if you'd obeyed orders and stayed put. But no, you just had to meddle and place yourself in danger."

She planted her hands on her hips. "Well excuse me for helping out a friend."

"You are not excused. You could have been killed," he grumbled.

"But I wasn't."

"By fluke."

"It wasn't fluke that took out the guys following me," she snapped, tired of him acting as if she were a useless girl. Partially her fault given she'd hidden her less-than-ladylike side from him all these years.

"You got lucky."

She growled. She couldn't help it. There was chauvinism, and then there was Boris. "I'll show you lucky." She stepped closer to him.

He frowned, but he held his ground as she invaded his space. "What do you think you are doing? I don't have time to play games, Jan. We need to call Reid and let him know you're safe."

"Only once you admit it."

"Admit what?" he asked with suspicion.

Admit you want me. Ha. Fat chance of that happening. One battle at a time. First things first. "Admit it was more than just luck."

Before he could reply, probably something that would irritate her to no end, she disarmed him. Stepping close, she placed her hands on his chest, smiled up at him sweetly, watched his eyes cloud in confusion—and then hooked his leg and shoved.

Had she not taken him by surprise, it probably wouldn't have worked, but Boris was so convinced she didn't have it in her that her trick worked.

Down he went, her atop him. He landed on his back with an "oomph," which might have had to do with the fact she brought her knee up against his chest to pin him. To keep him further off balance, she plastered her mouth to his.

Sweet electricity. Caught unaware, his lips were soft against hers, but nonetheless enjoyable. She almost forgot her main objective in the pleasure of finally touching him. Almost. But she'd spent too many years dealing with his moose-headedness.

She aimed the gun she pulled from his holster at his forehead and whispered against his mouth, "Bang. You're dead."

Chapter Four

I'm under attack!

Not from enemy fire, or a true foe, nothing more deadly than a ... kiss. A kiss that smashed through the walls he'd erected. An intimate press of lips that disarmed him completely and utterly. A sly ploy by a vixen who threatened him sweetly with his own gun.

"Still think it was a stroke of luck?" she asked in a playful tone.

If someone would have told him getting bested by a woman and threatened with his own weapon would turn him on, he would have punched them out. But that was before it happened to him.

Straddled by Jan's body, her face poised mere inches above his own, even the cold press of the barrel on his skin couldn't quell his erection.

I am a sick fuck. And a horny one. Didn't mean he'd do anything about it. His attraction to Jan, an attraction reciprocated, didn't change the situation. He still wasn't the right man for her.

No one is good enough for Jan. Which really sucked for her.

Still, the fact he couldn't have Jan—*along with anyone else*—didn't change the fact he needed to do something. They couldn't remain like this. *Well, we could, maybe with fewer clothes, more touching, more—*

Oops, strangle that thought. Focus. Boris could have easily taken the gun from her. If she intended to shoot, she would have by now, although he doubted she would and not just because the safety latch was still engaged. Little Jan was out to prove a point. Well dammit, she wasn't the only one who could prove something.

With reflexes born from necessity, Boris acted. It took only a heartbeat, or two, for him to grab her gun hand, hook his leg around her, flip their position so that he lay atop her—and for him to plunder her mouth.

She isn't the only one who can play dirty.

A long, long time ago, back when Boris still believed he could have a future with this stunning vixen, he'd kissed her. A kiss he'd relived over and over. A bright shining moment he'd used when despair threatened. He'd convinced himself over the years that the one embrace they'd shared surely wasn't so great. That he'd built up the pleasure of it in his mind.

Wrong.

If anything, the kiss they shared now was even more mind blowing than the first, or the second. As her soft lips tugged and teased his, as the wet tip of her tongue traced the seam of his mouth, he forgot what his plan was. Surely he'd had one when he'd decided to turn the tables?

Isn't the plan to kiss her senseless so she stops arguing? If so, he wasn't doing a great job because she murmured against his mouth, "Big cat, right behind you."

Fuck!

Boris rolled them both a moment before the large feline landed, claws extended, with a snarl. He could have blamed the cougar sneaking up on him on a multitude of things, such as the wind blowing in the wrong direction, but truth was, as usual, Jan distracted him. She took the edge off the predator in him, an edge that, as a moose, he fought hard to achieve.

Springing to his feet proved the proverbial red flag to their attacker. The cougar dove on him, sending them both crashing back to the ground. Calling his animal wasn't an option. While Boris could hold his own as a moose against many predators, when it came to close quarters and, for some reason felines, he fared better as a man.

Holding the snapping jaws from his face, he tucked his knees under the feline body and then pushed, heaving the shifter over his head to hit a rocky outcropping.

He heard clapping and turned incredulous eyes on Jan, the one making the noise.

"Not bad," she praised. "Although you lost some points on your tumble."

"Are you seriously judging my wrestling technique? You do know I served five years in the Marine Corps."

"And that makes you too good to be judged?" She shook her head. "Nope. If you get to judge me on the basis of my being a woman, then I get to grade you. Oh, you might want to look behind you before you fail."

Boris stepped to the side as the cat lunged. As the cougar soared past, he dove on its back.

"I'll have you know," he said with a grunt as he wrapped his arms around the furry neck. "That I once took on four cats at the same time and came out victorious."

"They were the normal household variety," Jan pointed out. "I've heard the story."

"They were Siamese and belonged to Aunt Betty-Sue. Ask anyone, those things are psycho. This guy, on the other hand," —Boris squeezed tighter and the feline went limp in his grip, a lack of oxygen making it pass out—"is easier to subdue than the Scorpii in the desert hills of the Mid-east."

"If you say so."

"I do. And I'm done." Boris stood and the cougar's subdued body dropped. He opted to not kill it, not with Jan watching. Despite her nonchalance over the violence, there was no sense in shocking her with an up-close death sentence to the enemy cat.

"Not done. We've got more company. Wolves."

Indeed. Boris could smell them coming. Feral wolves, again. Exactly how many of these did the enemy command? This kind of behavior was unnatural. However, the control someone exhibited over these wild ones skipped unnatural into downright unprecedented.

While he'd heard of some alpha lupines fooling the weaker ones in natural packs to follow, the numbers they'd already encountered, especially when you considered how many they'd killed, didn't make sense. *Where is our enemy getting them from?*

And how did he know to send them here?

Did it matter? The vicious canines bounded over the rocks and up the steep incline, nimble on their four paws. But they didn't catch

Boris unaware this time. He'd already stripped and shifted.

For this, he'd rely on his rack and his hooves to teach the small canine pack a lesson.

As he lowered his head to meet the charge from the first one, he noted Jan out of the corner of his eye taking aim and firing.

Well, at least she knows enough about guns to unclick the safety and aim. Judging by the yelp, she hit something too. Given how fast wolves could move, he doubted she'd landed a killing shot, but the loud noise would probably hold the rest at bay.

Then he couldn't worry about her as he dealt with the attacking dogs. Many people were under the mistaken impression moose were docile herbivores, big, lumbering, dumb giants.

Those people were the sticky stuff between his toes when he trampled their uneducated asses with his hooves. Moose—and before anyone asked, a group of them were not called meese—weren't the most aggressive of animals in the forest. They didn't have razor-sharp teeth, a vicious snarl, or pointed claws. But they were fucking strong with a rack that spanned up to six feet. They were also big, weighing in over seven hundred pounds. Piss one off and then imagine all that weight applied to a well-aimed stomp. However, his hooves weren't his only weapon. A whack from his antlers or a scoop, sweep, and fling also made for a great attack move.

In this situation, he relied on both those skills because Boris was annoyed. It was one thing for him to not want to kiss Jan; it was another to have some mangy wolves—who should have known better—interrupt it.

So he showed them the error of their ways, his limber joints allowing him to not only kick with his forelegs but his back ones too. Another benefit of his kind, he could even kick sideways.

In the zone, his mind cold and calculating, he took on the attacking gray wolves. He tossed them around like stuffed toys.

Until he heard Jan yell, "Ow, that hurt, you smelly mutt."

At that point he lost his mind and let out a roar that echoed.

If a moose could go ninja on some lupine asses, then that's what he did. No more Mr. Gentle Giant. His attack turned deadly. Forget kicking and tossing, he began stomping and crushing, biting anything furry that came within reach. He didn't move much, letting the furry ones come to him instead, lest the icy peak prove too much for four-legged footing. A proneness to broken legs was a moose's biggest fear and weakness.

When the area before him cleared, if one discounted the broken bodies, he tossed his antlered head and peered around for more of the enemy to play with. He even dragged a hoof through the snow and snorted, a warm steamy breath huffing from his nose.

Nothing left in front of him, but from behind, he felt a sharp sting as something chomped on his haunch.

Before he could kick out his leg and shake the mutt free, he heard a bang. The mouth clamped around his flesh loosened as the wolf attacking him hit the ground, dead.

Jan stood over the corpse and frowned. "Not even big enough for a good pair of mitts."

Morphing back to his man shape, because his moose vision sucked, he declared, "Wearing skin is wrong." As he said it, he took a peek around and noted the wolves were either littering the ground or limping off to lick their wounds. The cougar shifter he'd choked still drooled in the snow.

"It's only wrong if you buy it. There is nothing wrong with skinning something you've hunted and making use of it. If wolf flesh weren't so tough, I'd eat it too. Then again…" She tapped her chin in thought. "Think we can drag one back? I've got a recipe for stew I've been meaning to try."

Boris, in the process of dressing, shot her an incredulous gaze. "Like hell you'd eat it. I've seen your idea of lunch. Salads and fruit."

"Just making sure I eat healthily. And I'll have you know, I have a lot of meat in my diet. I might not have eaten much wolf meat, but I've partaken of my fair share of other prey. Stuff I've brought down. My daddy taught me not to waste what I hunt."

"Because you go hunting so often," he scoffed. Then again, maybe she did. Boris had done his best in the past few years to not pay attention to what the fox did during her time off. For all he knew, she liked to dance naked around bonfires. Now there was a visual to almost knock him to his knees, especially since he now had a clear image of what a naked Jan looked like.

Pale skin, rounded curves, fat pink nipples, blonde curls at the vee of her thighs. Good thing he'd already managed to get his pants on, or he'd have had a fine time explaining his sudden erection at the recollection of her sweet body.

The lack of weight in his empty holster reminded him to hold out his hand. "Now that the danger's passed, do you mind handing over my gun?"

She tucked it behind her back in a childish ploy. "Don't I get to keep it since I proved I can fire it without blowing off my own foot?"

"No." Sharing his gun was too much to ask. Sharing implied friendship, friendship led to conversation, conversation led to him grabbing her by the nape and dragging her in for another kiss.

And then ... bad things might happen. Even if they did have sex and it was great, nothing could come of it. He couldn't offer her the life she wanted, and he wouldn't lead her emotionally astray.

Because once upon a time I swore to beat the hell out of anyone who hurt her. Yet, if I'm the one dealing the pain, then that means I'd have to take care of myself. How would he explain that to his alpha?

Ignoring her angry look, he took the weapon she handed him and ejected the clip, replacing it with a fresh one. He then holstered it.

"Ready to go?" he asked as he threaded his arms through the straps on his pack. He eyed the unconscious cougar on the ground. Given he planned to question the feline, forget leaving him behind. Damn he looked heavy, though, and they had hours of trekking ahead of them. But he'd dragged bigger.

"Who says I want to go with you?" Her mutinous expression went well with her crossed arms.

This time, he didn't hold in his sigh. "Why are you testing me like this? What happened to nice Jan? The one who asks me if I want coffee?"

"That one is paid to serve java to idiots. I'm not on the clock now, and I see no reason to pander to your ego."

"My ego? What's asking if you're ready to go have to do with my ego?"

"Maybe I'm tired of trying to cater to you." She tilted her chin at a stubborn angle. "For years I've tried to play nice and get you to notice me. Well, no more, moosehead. From now on, no more Miss Nice Fox. Say hello to the real me. The not-so-nice vixen."

She wanted to be a bad vixen? He could have groaned, as that concept immediately had her dressed in his mind in tight latex with ruby red lips curved in a wicked smile as she crooked a finger at him. Fuck, there she went addling his brain again.

It drew a scowl from him and a mocking, "You don't have it in you to be bad." Too late, he recognized his challenge.

For the second time that day, she invaded his personal space, stepping right up to him to whisper across his lips. "And that just shows how little you know the real me, Boris."

His eyes went to half-mast as he waited for the inevitable kiss. Bad Jan would surely plant one to throw him off-kilter again. *But I'm ready for it this time.* As well as eager.

He almost cried out in protest when she stepped away and spun, coming face to face with a peeved cougar who'd woken from his nap sooner than expected.

Fuck me, I forgot to tie him up. Not his fault. Boris usually didn't make a practice of keeping people who attempted to kill him, alive.

He grabbed for his gun, determined to put an end to the damned cat who threatened his fox, only to discover his holster was once again empty. *Twice now she's taken my weapon.* Her and her damned feminine wiles!

Before he could demand she hand over his gun, Jan brought his gun up, two handed, and fired.

With a blink of its eyes, that didn't include the new third one in the middle of its forehead, the cougar toppled over. Dead.

Boris looked from the pile of fur to Jan, who chewed her lip in obvious annoyance, to the gun. "I can't believe you did that," he said. He couldn't. Despite the bodies he'd come across on his search, despite the story Reid once told him about Jan taking down a wild grizzly with nothing but a pocketknife and a slingshot, in spite of her comments, Boris never believed the elegant fox capable of such a deliberate and deadly act.

"Fudge it all, neither can I," Jan exclaimed.

"It's all right. You didn't have a choice," he soothed, somewhat placated by her finally normal response in killing something. An appropriate girly response to killing a cat who was a man.

Big eyes regarded him with incredulity. "You think I'm upset because he's dead?"

"It's okay to be. Killing isn't easy."

"I'm miffed because I should have aimed for his shoulder, because now how will we get some answers?" she said.

For real? She was worried about questioning the cougar who'd tried to impale him on his claws and stalked her for the last eight hours or more? "I'm sure Reid will have kept one of his cohorts alive."

"Reid's around here too?" she asked, peeking around. "I thought it was just you." Jan tucked his gun into the pocket of the large coat hanging on her frame. Given he had a few more stashed in his bag and in his boot, he decided let her keep it. She'd probably just steal it back again anyhow. At least he now knew she wouldn't shoot her toes off.

"Reid went after Tammy. According to my last text from him, they found her."

"She's all right?"

Boris shrugged. "I guess. He didn't really say."

"And did he take care of the thugs who took her?"

Yeah, led by none other than another old army buddy of theirs, Gene. Gene, whom they'd all thought dead in the prison camp they'd spent time in. The camp that forever changed his mental state and future.

"The guy leading them got away, but Reid and the boys managed to take several of the rogues down."

"Good."

The feral smile on her face should have shocked him, but Boris was beginning to realize that the Jan he knew wasn't the true Jan. The real Jan was a much tougher lady than he'd have ever credited. *Tough and sexy.*

For some reason he couldn't help but think this spelled big trouble. *And extreme pleasure.*

Speaking of Reid, though, and in need of distraction from the maddening vixen, he yanked out his cell phone and put a call in to Reid. As alpha of the clan, he'd want to know Boris had located Jan.

He didn't bother with pleasantries when Reid answered. "I found her."

"Jan? She's okay?"

Before Boris could reply, Jan snatched the phone out of his hand. "Is that the boss? Let me talk to him."

"Give that back, woman."

"Make me."

"Since when did you get so argumentative?"

'Weren't you paying attention before? Since a moose decided I wasn't good enough for him."

"I never said that."

But Jan ignored him to answer Reid's earlier question. "Of course, I'm fine. No thanks to big dumbass here, tromping around like, well, a big ol' moose and leading the enemy right to me."

"I took care of them," Boris said, a tad defensively. Had she not disarmed him with a kiss in the first place, he'd have probably spotted the cougar sneaking up on them and the wolves and... Okay, so he was off his game today.

"With my help," she corrected.

"Taking down one wolf doesn't constitute help."

"It does if it's trying to chew your leg off," she retorted.

"You're trying my patience, woman," Boris grumbled, crossing his arms and glaring at her.

"I've already told you where to shove that. Would you like help?" Jan asked sweetly.

He showed her what she could do with her offer.

"I assume that waggling finger means no? Then, in that case, if you don't mind, I'm talking to my boss. A civilized man. A man who isn't afraid to go after what he wants, unlike certain people."

His brows drew together. "Are you calling me a coward?"

Her lips curved into a taunting smirk. "Yes. I'm also willing to find some yellow paint and smear your belly with it."

"I am not afraid," he yelled. Once again, she had him losing his temper.

"Oops, I think Reid hung up on me."

"Who can blame him? You're irrational. I don't know how the man works with you."

Tossing him his phone, Jan smirked. "Maybe if you tried me on for size, you'd *appreciate* my merits."

Yeah, he didn't miss the innuendo. Yeah, he wanted to try her on—the tip of his dick especially wanted to wear her. But he wouldn't let her goad him into acting. "Your plan to get me to sleep with you won't work."

"If you say so, mouse." And with that saucy insult, she skipped down the steep slope, heading back the way they'd come.

Did she just call me mouse? Why did she deliberately taunt him? But more importantly, why did it turn him on?

Chapter Five

Jan was fully aware she'd pushed Boris to his limits. Only a completely oblivious person could miss his very obvious displeasure. She didn't care that he simmered or that he grumbled under his breath. His glares amused her because, despite it all, it meant *he* noticed.

Notices me.

Once upon a time, Jan might have felt bad about how she treated him, except … for the first time in years she was having fun. Forget hiding behind some sweet veneer, acting like a lady in the hopes Boris would come to the realization she was the peanut butter missing on his jelly sandwich. The glue he needed to piece his life together. Acting that way had gotten her nowhere. So she was done. No more bending over backwards trying to please him. Her new motto? *Take me as I am, or stuff it.*

Wonder of all wonders, it took her showing her true bossy self for him to finally take note. And when she'd dared to give him a kiss in the hopes of jolting him, she'd gotten more than she could have ever hoped for.

He kissed me back! Quite ardently too. As a matter of fact, he'd not quite managed to hide his arousal ever since the moment he'd laid eyes on her naked frame.

If I'd known all it would take was a striptease, attitude, and a smooch to get him to acknowledge I'm alive, I'd have done it years ago. However, now that she'd finally garnered some interest, she had to tread with care because, despite her belief Boris and she were meant to become mates, it didn't mean he wouldn't bolt or try to retreat behind the shell he'd erected around his emotions. Either was a distinct possibility, so she had to look out for herself, which meant not allowing him to tread on her emotions or ignore her again.

Nope. Time to hold her head high and stop her pitiful attempts to gain his interest. If the moose wanted Jan, he'd have to prove it. She was done chasing him. He knew what she wanted. Now, it was up to him to lay claim.

If he could catch her. Her human form might not have the sleek agility of her fox, but she was still quite nimble, and unburdened, she skipped along while he trudged in his snowshoes. Instinct guided her feet away from the drifts that would have bogged her steps. They encountered no wild animals or mishaps on their return trip, which took less time, given they could make a straight beeline to his truck instead of the weaving path she'd taken in an attempt to lose her pursuers.

It wasn't until they'd clambered into his vehicle and were heading back home that Boris— her sexy and sulky moose—finally deigned to speak to her. Course, it wasn't a declaration of love, but it was a start.

"Back on that hill, you said something about your daddy taught you to hunt?"

"He did."

"With a gun?"

She laughed. "Gun. Sling shot. Arrows. Four feet. Traps. My daddy always wanted a boy, but he got me instead. Lucky for him, I didn't mind learning what he had to teach. We spent hours in the woods together with him teaching me everything he knows about surviving in the wild."

"But you're so ... so ..."

"Girly?" She smiled. "That would be my momma's influence. As her only daughter, she made sure I didn't turn into a tomboy."

"How did I never know this about you?" He seemed genuinely perturbed, or so she surmised by his creased brow.

"Probably because you never bothered to ask. You just assumed you knew the real me. It's a mistake many people make." Although, anybody who grew up with her knew of her less-than-dainty side. How amusing no one bothered to clue him in. Then again, Boris, since his return from the war, didn't exactly encourage male bonding.

"Girls who bring homemade brownies to work with icing smiley faces and who wear pearls and heels aren't exactly girls who usually track wild animals and carve them up for their pelt and dinner."

"I'm special."

"You're special all right," he grumbled. He changed the subject. "So how many guns do you have?"

"Why not come over one night and find out?" Yes, she added a husky lilt to the invitation.

He shot her down and didn't even bother to pretend he didn't grasp her implied intent. "Despite what happened on that hill, nothing has changed."

She sighed at his quick rejection. "I didn't think anything had."

"I'm not your mate."

She didn't reply. Why bother? He'd deny the truth. She'd feel a pang of hurt. Then once again, she'd curse the war that changed the boy she first fell for into a man scared of happiness.

After that, they fell into a stilted silence. Although, more than once, from the corner of her eye, she caught him staring at her, his jaw moving as if he meant to speak but couldn't find the words. Boris off balance. About time.

When they reached her house in town, she hopped out of his truck before he could make it around. Judging by the tic in his jaw, he didn't like this continued reminder that she didn't actually need him.

"Thanks for bringing me back," she said, turning her back on him

Despite her dismissal, he still walked her to the door and, even once she let herself in, he didn't leave. Standing in the doorframe, his massive shoulders practically touching each side, his expression confused, he managed to murmur, "I guess I'll be seeing you around."

Not with that lack of enthusiasm he wouldn't. "Or not," she said tartly before closing the door in his face.

Rude, perhaps, but enjoyable. A nice girl would have thanked him for taking the time to come to her rescue, even if she was doing fine on her own. A nice girl might have even hugged or perhaps kissed him again in the hopes of triggering a heated, "You're welcome". But Jan was a fox, and as her father always reminded her, a fox's true strength lay in their ability to be wily.

Time to put her strengths to use.

The next day, Jan went to work as if she hadn't spent almost the entire previous day wandering the frozen tundra. Reid didn't bat an eye at her return. They'd more or less grown up together, despite their gap in age. He had a sister Jan hung out with, so he was fully aware that a day spent in the wild was a walk in the park compared to the weeklong trips her dad used to take her on. But, in a surprising twist, Boris came to the company head office looking for Reid. Rare because he tended to avoid the times Jan worked. He usually showed up after hours or when she skipped out for lunch.

For a man determined to pretend she didn't exist, he was pretty knowledgeable about her schedule.

He couldn't hide his surprise when he lumbered in. He barked, "What the hell are you doing here, woman? You should be at home recovering."

"Recovering from what?" she asked as she stood with a file in need of putting away. "I only suffered minor abrasions and bruises, which are mostly gone already."

"But what about your mental state?"

"What about it?"

"You were attacked."

"I was."

"You killed some men."

"I did."

"Doesn't it bother you?"

Not really, but she could see it bothered him. She caught his eye. "Listen, I'm not going to lie and say I enjoyed doing what I did. No one ever enjoys taking a life. But I'm also not a fool. It was either me or them. When it comes to survival, I can and will do what it takes. Just like you did what you had to while overseas."

"That was different."

"Why, because you're a man?"

"No, because it was war, and I knew I'd have to kill."

"And those men attacked me and destroyed my truck. If you ask me, they deserved worse than a swift death."

He practically choked. "I don't know who you are anymore."

She fixed him with an enigmatic smile. "Probably because you never did. You never gave me a chance."

"Because I can't. I'm not the man you think I am."

"No, you're not the man *you* think you are. I see you perfectly fine."

"I'm damaged, Jan."

"So let me help fix that."

"It's not that simple."

Because he wouldn't allow it. "Chicken."

"Stop it. It's not going to work."

There was that special tick in his jaw again. Good. It meant she was hitting a nerve. She smirked. "I get it. Don't moose with you." Yes, she totally went there, and snickered while doing it. His incredulous expression was totally worth the bad pun.

"Are you mocking me?"

"Who me?" She batted her lashes in false innocence. "Would I do such a thing?"

He frowned. "A day or so ago, you wouldn't have dared."

"A day or so ago, I still gave a damn about what you thought. And that wasn't the real me. Not that you'd know, since you scurry away like a mouse before a fox every time I enter the room."

"Do not."

"Do to. Name the last time we were both alone together."

"Yesterday."

She snorted. "Before that."

His lips tightened into a thin line.

"You can't, can you, because you haven't allowed yourself to spend any time with me. Admit it, you're scared of me."

"I am not scared. I just don't like clingy women."

Her eyes widened. "Clingy? You did not just seriously call me that."

"I made myself clear I wasn't interested, but you kept throwing yourself at me. What's a man supposed to do?"

Way to make her sound desperate. Well, he wouldn't have to worry about that anymore. She was done trying to please him. "Nothing apparently. Except stew in his own misery. But don't worry. I'm done chasing after a bullheaded moose. I'm moving onto other pastures and other men, ones that don't mind grazing."

"What's that supposed to mean?" His expression darkened.

"It means, since you don't want me, I'm going to find a man who does."

"About time. A girl like you needs a man to take care of her."

Funny how he said it with a twist of his lips as if the idea seemed distasteful.

"First off, I can take care of myself. And what do you mean about time? You didn't seriously think I spent the last few years staying home alone pining after you?" Judging by his expression, he had. She snorted. "Sorry to disappoint you, big guy, but despite my erroneous belief you're my mate, I've been with other men." More in an attempt to salve her wounded ego at Boris's continued rejection. "So if you're harboring some delusion that I've been a cloistered virgin these past few years, hate to disappoint you."

She'd not meant to speak so bluntly, but after years of dancing around, it was time to lay things out in the open. She was tired of watching her friends hook up. Tired of waiting. Tired of being alone.

And once again, the truth had unexpected results.

Chapter Six

Jan's been with other men.

The air practically whooshed from him at Jan's admission. The revelation hit Boris harder than a well-aimed fist to his gut. In the years he'd fought to ignore her, to pretend he didn't feel the same attraction, he'd assumed so much. Assumed for example that she did wait on him and him alone. Assumed she didn't look at or touch another. But as her words filtered, jealously burned, bright and hot. "As if I care who you're dating." *Tell me who and I'll strangle him with my bare hands.*

"Dating?" She laughed. "I don't know if I'd call it that."

"Seeing someone stead then."

"I'm not seeing anyone at all. Haven't for a while." She shrugged. "As a woman, I have needs and I'm not ashamed to satisfy them with whoever's handy. Sometimes I'll keep him around for a while if he's good. Other times, I just take what he offers then move on."

He might need help picking his jaw off the floor. "You've been sleeping around?"

"Not really sleeping. Oh, don't tell me you're shocked. What did you expect? You made it clear for years I was mistaken about you. Did you really think I'd stay a spinster forever? Or that I'd really spend all my time mooning over the picture I have of you?"

Startled, he said, "You have a picture of me?"

"Yes I do but don't change the subject. I have a healthy sexual appetite, and the fact you refuse to satisfy it doesn't mean I went hungry. Besides, don't tell me you are purer than newly fallen snow. I hear you're quite the lady's man when you go into the city with your buddies."

She heard about that? Heat suffused his cheeks, a heat he'd not felt in years. Surely not embarrassment? What did he have to feel ashamed about? It wasn't as if he owed her anything. And yet, he still found himself defending his actions. "That's different."

"How?"

"Because I'm a man." Yeah. He went there. But, in his defense, he didn't grunt or scratch when he said it.

Didn't matter. She acted as if he did. A disdainful snort scrunched her perfect features, and damn her if she still wasn't gorgeous.

"You're a prehistoric cave moose, and I'm done having you judge me. If you'll excuse me, I have better things to do." She turned her back on him, dismissing him.

As if there was anything better than doing him.

Good thing he didn't say that aloud. Even in his head, it screamed sexual innuendo.

Unsure of a reply, he should have fled, but that smacked too much of letting her win, given she'd tossed the last words.

So he stood there, trying to think of something clever to say that didn't scream, "I'm a dick". Probably too late.

He tracked her with his gaze as Jan went to the filing cabinet in the corner of the room and bent over. Her ass thrust into the air, her dress slacks hugging the rounded curve of her buttocks, fixating him. Rousing him.

Unfair! How dare she play dirty and tease him like that?

Boris couldn't have said how he ended up across the room behind her. All he knew was, when Jan straightened and whirled with a gasp, she stood in his space, close enough for him to smell her sweet perfume.

He couldn't resist.

With less-than-gentle hands, he grabbed her about the waist and hoisted her to his lips.

"What are you doing?" she demanded, her voice low and husky.

"Getting the last word in," he murmured against her mouth. Then he took her lips, branding them with a kiss, determined to erase the memories of those who'd touched them before.

She's mine.

For once, he didn't refute the claim. For once, he reveled in the thought. Allowed it to override common sense.

He pressed her closer, molding her body to his, every sweet curve, curves he'd dreamed of. As his lips devoured hers, he forgot his reasons for staying away or even the fact he'd begun the embrace to get even.

Until she bit him.

With a curse, he pulled back. "What the fuck was that for?"

"I never gave you permission to kiss me," was her prim reply.

"Since when do I have to ask?"

"Since I decided you're right, you're not the man for me. Now, if you'll unhand me, I have work to do."

He almost echoed the mournful mental bellow of his moose as he released her, her warmth fleeing as she stepped away.

For a moment, he almost reached out to tuck her back. Almost. In that moment, he might have done something foolish had she given him the slightest encouragement.

She didn't. In fact, she didn't deign to look at him or address him as she returned to her desk. The vixen dismissed him in spite of the fact her lips were full and red from their embrace. She ignored him as if he couldn't scent the perfume of her arousal.

She desires me and yet she pushed me away.

Exactly what he wanted, so why did it piss him off?

With a grumbled curse, Boris spun on a heel and left. Forget the reason why he'd come to the office in the first place. He couldn't stay another minute. Not if he wanted to retain what little sanity he had left.

Ha. Too late. It was obvious he wasn't working with a full deck, or he would have never kissed her in the first place. Or second. Heck, if he wasn't careful, he'd end up with a hat-trick.

Not if I can avoid her.

And he did. Boris stayed away from the tempting vixen. He volunteered for all the patrols guarding the clan from rogue intrusions.

Accompanied as many truck runs into the city as he could. He stayed well away from the vixen, all under the guise of helping the clan out. In reality, he was hiding.

Yeah, he hid, mostly from his own feelings, but he was also protecting Jan … from him.

His dreams took on a frightening twist. The nightmares of the time he'd spent while in the 'tender' care of his captors overseas now featured Jan. Jan in their clutches. Jan screaming in pain and terror. A Jan he couldn't save, just like he couldn't save so many of his friends and fellow soldiers.

He awoke from those ghastly nightmares clicking an imaginary gun, a cold and clammy sweat bathing his body. No matter his desire for her, he couldn't subject her to this. Jan deserved a man less broken. A man she could sleep with at night. *A better man than me.*

Altruism sucked.

His mission to avoid the perturbing vixen was going well until one Saturday, when she should have been anywhere but the office. As he left Reid's inner sanctum, he practically ran her over.

"What are you doing here?" he snapped, caught off guard and not liking it one bit. His racing heart had little to do with shock but everything to do with her. He quenched his need for her, a thirst that almost drove him insane, by taking in her appearance.

Dressed casually in jeans and a clingy sweater, even at her most relaxed, Jan exuded elegance. It was hard to reconcile the current Jan with the feisty vixen he'd encountered in the wild a few weeks back. There were times he wondered if he'd imagined the rougher, more capable Jan.

"What do you mean, what am I doing here? I work here."

"It's the weekend," he pointed out.

"And we have a shipment scheduled to arrive. I wanted to be on hand since Gary's home sick and unable to itemize the stock."

How delicious and perfect she looked, her smell still so utterly tantalizing. He wanted to rub his face in the silky softness of her hair. Butt his head against her in affection. Claim those pink—

A mental shake freed him from the direction of those thoughts, and he dropped his gaze, lest he get mesmerized by her again. But it wasn't her eyes that snared him but a bulge at her side, hidden by her top.

What's this?

Without thinking or asking, he reached out to lift her shirt for a peek.

She slapped at his hand. "Excuse me, but what do you think you're doing?"

Shocked at her action, he withdrew his hand and said, "You slapped me."

"It's usually the correct response when a guy tries to cop a feel."

"I wasn't copping a feel."

"Says the guy who was trying to stick his hand up my shirt. Count yourself lucky I left my knife in my coat, or you might have lost some fingers." She said it with a smile, but surely she didn't mean it.

Did she?

Jan threatening bodily harm. It shouldn't have been a turn-on, and yet, as with everything else about her, it was. He tried to keep his mind on track. "Is that a gun you're hiding under there?"

"Yes." She didn't elaborate, instead completing his action, raising her sweater high enough to show him the supple fabric holster strapped against her skin, the butt of a pistol peeking from it.

Say what you would, but a woman wearing a gun was sexy, and Jan sporting one, nestled against her creamy skin? Boris swallowed hard.

One good thing about his ridiculous obsession with Jan? He was saving a ton of money lately with all the cold showers he was taking. "Why are you wearing a gun?"

"Because, despite the lack of recent attacks, a girl can never be too safe."

"I've never seen you wear one before."

She shrugged. "It depends on my outfit. Some accommodate it without ruining the line. With other ensembles, it's better to have the gun in my purse. Given there's not a lot of folk around on a Saturday, I thought it best to keep it handy. You never know when you might have to shoot a varmint."

And yes, she stared right at him as she said it.

"Good idea."

"I'm so glad you approve," was her sarcastic reply.

"I guess I should go." He said it; he just didn't move.

"You should." She didn't move either.

In silence they regarded each other, a taut standoff that could explode if not treated with care. It figured she'd be the one to pull the pin holding his emotional grenade in check.

She didn't say a word; she didn't have to. Her lips curved into a knowing smirk, one that said, 'I know you want me, you yellow-bellied moose'.

Damn her, he did. And damn her, he couldn't stop himself from a sudden need to wipe that smirk away, and what better way than with his mouth?

So much for keeping his distance. He yanked her into his arms and plastered his lips against hers, a man starved for her touch and feeding the hunger only she could sate.

A kiss. Only a kiss. The most deadly kiss he'd ever known.

Once again, reason, excuses, everything got swept away in the taste of her. The feel of her. His need for this vixen.

If only she would protest his manhandling of her. Or push him away. Something. Anything to stop him, because Boris was too weak to resist. The rebels and their torturous methods could have taken lessons from Jan because she killed him, not with violence or pain but gentleness and acceptance.

His hands, gripping her waist, skimmed upward, sliding under the hem of her shirt, the silky smoothness of her skin like cashmere against his calloused fingertips. The hitch of her breath was surely the sexiest sound on this earth.

He reveled in the embrace. How he'd missed and longed for this closeness. How he'd missed her witty repartee, her scent, her—

The opening of a door provided the rude awakening and reminder they were in a public place, doing things he'd vowed never to do, not even in private.

He separated from her as rapidly as possible, but not quick enough to miss the mirth-filled gaze of Reid, his alpha.

"Should I come back later?" Reid asked with an arched brow.

Before Boris could reply, Jan did. "No. We were done here. Boris was just leaving."

I am?

Yeah, he was. But not because she said so. He had other things to do. Important things he was sure to recall once he unscrambled his flustered mind. "I'll see you later." He didn't specify who because he might have lied and said Reid, when in reality the one he wanted to see was Jan.

Yes, I'd love to see her. Naked and in my bed.

Thank fuck for the cold temperature outside. It helped to cool his ardor as he emerged from the building. Standing in front of the company headquarters, he took a few deep, calming breaths.

What the fuck happened to me in there?

Was he doomed to kiss the damned woman every time he went near her? If that was the case, he'd really have to work harder on avoiding her.

Yellow-bellied coward. Yes, those words rang in his mind in Jan's accusatory voice. He didn't care. This bullheaded moose wasn't about to let a few sweet kisses change his mind. Sweet embraces changed nothing. Boris wasn't the man for Jan.

A few more deep lungfuls of sharp, crisp air later and he felt ready to go when he caught motion from the corner of his eye. Not a big deal, except for the fact it was man-shaped and furtive.

In a town of several hundred, there were no real strangers and everyone said hello. Even if you'd banged a guy's sister and never called her back and he hated your freaking guts, you said "Hey". Poor Rodney got more than his fair share of fat lips trying to defend his sister's nonexistent honor.

But back to who would be lurking in the parking lot. If this were high school, he'd think it was smoking teens. If this were anywhere but Beark Enterprises, with Reid in the office, he'd think it was some dock workers sharing a reefer. However, on the outskirts of town, placing it close to the mine, and with vacant acres around should they need to expand, the company wasn't exactly a hotspot for traffic of any kind.

Given the trouble they'd encountered with a certain discontented shifter, intent on causing havoc with the clan, Boris didn't think he should take chances.

With long strides, the only kind an almost seven foot man ever took, he crossed the parking lot, the dawning dark enough to cast deep shadows and force him to strain his eyes. He didn't spot any more motion, but he did catch the lingering fresh scent of ... flowers? In the deep of winter?

Brow creased, he peeked around, sniffing to pinpoint the source, which turned out to be the front seat of an SUV. Not just any SUV. Jan's.

What the hell?

He yanked the door handle to her truck, which opened because no one in these parts ever bothered locking them. In a neat, thick bundle on the front seat lay a bouquet of red roses.

What the fuck?

Who the hell is leaving my vixen flowers? Did she have a boyfriend? A lover…

Suddenly enraged, he grabbed the bundle and strode back to the office, not pausing to analyze his actions or why he felt like swapping skins to let his rampaging moose out to find someone to toss in the air and skewer on his rack. Never mind his antlers didn't have the sharpest of tines. He'd make it work even if he had to pin the bastard to a wall and slam the blunt tip against him a few times to impale him.

Yeah!

Slamming the outer door shut, then the inner door of the office, he stomped his way back in, only to halt mid-step as Jan barked, "Dry those boots off, mister, or remove them. I will not slip in puddles because you lack manners."

To think he'd erroneously thought her docile. He growled as, with great exaggeration, he scuffed his snowy boots whilst holding the bouquet aloft.

She arched a brow. "That better not be for me."

"I will damn well growl at you if I like," he said, still in a very growly kind of mood.

"You'll what? I meant—Oh never mind."

Feet dried, he tramped his way to her desk and slapped the fragrant flowers down, sending wilted petals scattering onto her desk. Keeping flowers fresh this time of year and out here wasn't easy. In spite of their sad state, whoever got them must have paid a pretty penny, the fucking jerk. "Care to explain this?"

She cast a glance at the bouquet. "They're flowers. Roses to be exact."

"And who are they from?"

"Doesn't matter, because I don't want them."

"Why not? They're from your boyfriend," he snapped.

Her face brightened, and Boris felt a pang of hurt at her obvious joy at the mention of the man he so wanted to kill. "My boyfriend? Is that what you're calling yourself now?" she asked with a smile.

Say what? "Me? I'm not your bloody boyfriend. I'm talking about the secretive bastard who left these in your truck. You could have told me before I kissed you that you were seeing somebody."

The joy lighting her face extinguished, and it didn't take long for him to grasp the misunderstanding as she said, "I don't have a boyfriend, and if you aren't the one who bought me these flowers, then I have no idea what or whom you're talking about."

"So you don't have a boyfriend?" he repeated. It didn't escape him that when she'd thought he referred to himself she'd seemed more than happy.

"I wouldn't have kissed you if I did," she retorted. "I might have a sexually healthy appetite, but I'm not a two-timing light skirt."

"But then who are these from?" he asked, perversely pleased at Jan's single state.

"How would I know? I've never seen them before. First I heard of them was when you threw them on my desk. You said you found them in my truck? What were you doing snooping in it?"

"I wasn't snooping. I saw something suspicious and investigated."

"Of course, because rare blooms are so dangerous." She rolled her eyes.

"Stop mocking me."

"Then stop acting like a donkey instead of a moose."

Before they got further off track, he jabbed a finger at the wilting foliage. "So you don't know who they're from?"

"Not yet. But I intend to find out." Then, in a move women everywhere must have bargained for with the devil, she proceeded to put his sleuthing skills to shame and make him look like an ass—instead of a moose—by pulling out an envelope tucked amidst the leaves.

A less-than-rational part of him thought he should grab it and read it first. And then hunt down the guy who left it, beat him to a pulp and teach him to poach a moose's vixen.

The cold soldier who'd learned to compartmentalize throttled that impulse and watched dispassionately—with fists clenched—as she opened it, read it, and gasped.

Chapter Seven

Elation to dismay, and all in the space of minutes.

Talk about a roller coaster of emotions. When Boris stalked back in bearing a bouquet of roses and tossed them on her desk claiming they were from her boyfriend, for one brief shining moment, she'd actually thought he meant himself. That in the past few weeks, where their glimpses of each other proved scarce because Boris kept himself busy with out-of-town trips, he'd had time to think things over. Surely he'd relived the kisses they'd shared. The passion that simmered. Like her, he must feel the magnetic draw between them.

Not even close. She'd misconstrued his words. He wasn't declaring himself with the flowers. He was accusing her … of what exactly? You couldn't cheat on someone who didn't belong to you.

Striving to keep a hold of her emotions, Jan distracted herself by plucking free the card in the leaves and reading the note.

A gasp escaped her. "Oh, how romantic."
Roses are red, snow is pure white,
As a vixen you are stunning,
One day you'll be my wife.
Signed, *Your Ghostly admirer.*

The missive was practically ripped from her grip as Boris grabbed it. He scanned it, his lips tightening, his brow creasing, a rumble shaking his frame. In that moment, he was more animal than man. So sexy. Especially since she finally grasped the reason for his rage—jealousy.

Ha. You might be trying to ignore me, but only because you care.

"Who is this from?" he demanded.

"I don't know, but I like his style."

"You like a criminal who breaks into your SUV and leaves you a stalker's manifesto!"

She couldn't help it, she laughed. "Stalker's manifesto?" The more he glowered, the harder she chortled.

"This isn't funny, Jan. Aren't you disturbed at all that some guy has been spying on you and is fixated enough to break into your truck and threaten to marry you?"

"It's a poem, Boris, not a bomb. And yes, I do think it's sexy." She combed fingers through her hair. "I wonder who it is? Maybe that hot new guy they hired to run the mine? I hear he's single."

"You shouldn't date company workers," Boris blurted.

She waved a negligent hand. "Bah. The mine is technically a whole other company. And besides, Reid never made that a formal policy. It's more of a if-you-date-and-break-up,-either-learn-to-work-together-or-I'll-fire-you kind of thing."

"If this new mine manager is so goddamned hot, then why didn't he bring the flowers to you in person?"

"Maybe he's shy," she mused, stifling a giggle at his grumbles. Yes, she delighted in torturing him. Who would have thought a jealous Boris would prove so fun, and sexy.

"Or it's not one of the townsfolk at all. Maybe it's a trap to get you to let down your guard."

"What are you talking about?"

"I only know of one guy with the nickname Ghost. Gene."

"Gene, your old army buddy? The one you all thought was dead who was harassing Reid?"

"The one and only."

"But why would he target me? I've never even met the man."

"How the hell would I know why? The guy's fucking crazy. Just because Gene and his gang have been lying low since the incident doesn't mean they're done. Maybe this is a ploy."

"A ploy? To do what? Deprive Reid of the best secretary and personal assistant a man could ask for?"

"To get at me."

Jan blinked. "Get at you? How is leaving me flowers attacking you?"

"Because."

Boris might not say it, but given his actions recently, Jan could guess. In denial or not, Boris cared about her. Cared enough that this Gene person, if he was indeed spying and out for revenge, might think that, by acting against Jan, he'd hurt Boris.

Awesome. But how to get Boris to admit it? "Or maybe you're just paranoid. I am single after all. Is it so farfetched to believe a man might want to do something romantic like leave me flowers?"

"Until we know for sure, you need protection."

"I've got protection right here." She patted her holstered gun.

"Not good enough. I'm in town for the next few days until the next truck run goes out. I guess I'll have to stick close to you and make sure there's no threat."

If he'd said it without a moue of distaste, she might have felt a spurt of pleasure, or hope. But no, he had to look as if he sucked a lemon. Jerk. "Oh no you don't. I don't need your big clunky moose self getting in my way. Why, if you're glued to me, however will my secret admirer make his next move?"

"Exactly."

Despite her protests, Boris remained nearby. He glowered from a corner in the warehouse as she ticked off an item list against the most recent delivery. He sulked in a chair in the office as she caught up on email. He shadowed her in his truck as she drove to the grocery store. And when he followed her inside? She made him pay by stooping often to snag items she didn't really need from low shelves.

Her antics didn't result in another impromptu kiss, but they had an effect judging by the simmering heat in his gaze whenever her eyes met his.

Once she reached her place, as she opened the back of her SUV to grab her groceries, he was there, taking the bags from her.

"I can carry them myself."

"Don't argue. Open the damned door so you stop making a target of yourself."

Yes, because her townhouse in the middle of town was so likely to come under attack. Given

Boris' rapier-like watch of the shadows, which stretched in the waning daylight, he thought it possible.

She unlocked her door and let them in. He kicked off his boots without being told and in stocking clad feet—practical wooly ones with reinforced toes—carried her bags to the kitchen and deposited them on the counter. Mission accomplished, she expected him to leave. Instead, he roamed her space, looking behind furniture, inside closets.

"What are you doing?" she asked.

"Guarding you."

"Can't you do that from outside?" Because, despite the openness of her kitchen, his size dwarfed it and made her all too aware of him. While she would welcome a repeat kiss—or more—she didn't want to be the one tempted into giving in first. She meant what she'd said and promised herself before. If Boris wanted her, he'd have to prove it.

But, then again, a little nudge or push wouldn't hurt. Unless he was on the edge of a cliff. She'd reserve that for later if his stubbornness proved too much.

"I need to make sure no one's infiltrated your home."

She could have told him no one had. Nothing got by her sharp nose. But, if it made him feel better, let the man skulk. She'd just finished putting away her groceries when he hit the stairs to check out the second floor.

Her inner vixen perked up. *He's going to be in my bedroom.* It was too good an opportunity to ignore. She caught him as he exited her en suite, sensed him really, as she had her rear end facing the door and felt the skin of her bare back tingle.

"What are you doing?" he asked, his voice rougher than usual.

She cast him a coy glance over her shoulder. "Taking off my shirt."

"Jan, I know that kiss from earlier was probably confusing. But nothing has changed."

She laughed. "You think I'm stripping for you?" She whirled around, clad in her jeans, bra, and holster. "Sorry to disappoint, big guy. I'm just taking this sucker off. It's all well and good to wear my gun in public, but I'm home now, and I've got weapons stashed all over the place. So might as well get comfortable." Holding his gaze, she skimmed her hands over her body to undo the clasps holding it in place.

He visibly swallowed. "Do you have to do that in front of me?"

Yes. She liked the fact he couldn't tear his eyes from her. "Don't tell me I'm making you uncomfortable? We're shifters. We see naked people all the time."

"But they're not you."

The words were practically whispered, and for a moment, she thought she'd imagined them, except Boris practically ran from her room, his heavy steps tramping down the stairs. The slam of the door followed only a moment after.

Jan smiled. *I will outfox you yet, my big moose.*

Chapter Eight

Someone looked like the devil chased him.
A devil or was he haunted by a ghost?

Gene hadn't acquired his nickname by chance. He truly was a ghost, able to drift into places unseen, unheard, all but invisible until he decided to show himself.

Now wasn't one of those times. Camped in the vacant apartment across the street from a certain female fox, the occupants gone on an extended cruise, Gene had the perfect spot to watch, wait, and plot his next move.

He'd had his fun with Reid, that Kodiak bastard, and his mate. He wasn't quite done with him, but given the alpha's watchful eyes since their encounter, Gene backed off. He'd let the big bear off the hook for the moment and lull him into a false sense of safety. Then he'd strike again when he least expected it.

In the meantime, though, there were other people to target. More *old friends*, men he'd trusted to have his back. Men he, once upon a time, would have laid his life down for. Men who'd left him behind when they escaped the cesspool and assholes holding them prisoner.

It didn't matter in Gene's mind that they thought him dead.

They left me.

Left him to suffer. Alone. In pain.

Even now, Gene still felt the lingering effects of the torture they'd subjected him to, and he'd probably never rid himself of the nightmares.

But he could share them. He'd spent a lot of time watching those who'd made it back. Spied as they settled into the quaint and remote town of Kodiak Point. With its shifter friendly population, and most of the men he'd once served with—those that survived at any rate—in residence, he could have happily lived.

Now he happily plotted. His next victim? None other than a moose. *My old friend, Boris.*

Hurting Boris initially seemed impossible, short of a head-on confrontation, until certain rumors he'd gleaned from social media sites and the moose's actions themselves confirmed it.

Boris had the hots for Jan, a blonde arctic fox. The same Jan whose picture Boris used to keep in his pocket back when they served together. The Jan who Boris now studiously avoided. A fox he'd seen the moose kiss through a telescopic lens when he'd spied on them through the windows of Beark Enterprises.

It gave Gene an idea.

The roses and the note caused some decent fireworks, or so his planted bug indicated. Gene quite enjoyed the moose's jealous fit. It just cemented Gene's belief that, to truly hit Boris where it would hurt, he needed to do what the moose feared most.

Pretend to steal his woman, and if that didn't work, threaten her.

Once upon a time, Gene would have never harmed a hair on a female's head. That was before he learned sadism wasn't an exclusively male gene.

And as Boris slammed his way out of the vixen's house, Gene smiled. Time to fuck with a moose by playing with his fox.

Chapter Nine

Drumming his fingers on the dash of his truck, Boris mentally castigated himself for running away. What sane man took off like a mouse before an owl when faced with a sexy woman wearing a bra?

I did.

Because if he hadn't, she wouldn't have worn that bra—which cupped her supple breasts so perfectly—for long.

Did fleeing make him a smart man or the biggest wuss in town? Not a question he'd pose to any of his guy friends, that was for sure. He preferred to keep his man card and wouldn't want to kill any of his buds just for deservedly mocking him.

And mock him they would. Jan was simply a cute little fox. Nothing dangerous or menacing about her, despite her predilection for guns and her fearlessness when it came to violence. So what if she didn't even scream like a girl when she killed things? She didn't pose a real danger.

Unless the danger of losing his heart counted.

But Boris wasn't about to allow her to steal that part of him. He kept what was left of the damaged organ safely locked away.

Oh yeah, if my heart's so secure, then why the hell am I parked outside her place?

For protection.

Against what? A possible secret admirer?

Yes. Any man without the balls to ask her out to her face didn't deserve her. The fact that wasn't his choice to make didn't enter the equation.

Boris felt a responsibility toward Jan. A lifetime ago, he had led her to believe they'd share something when he got back from the war because when he left, bright-eyed and fuzzy-racked, he'd totally intended to. Then shit happened.

It wasn't her fault he couldn't keep that whispered promise, but he could at least ensure that until she found a man to replace him—grrrr…—that she was well protected and—

What the fuck is she doing on her front porch wearing only a towel and aiming a gun? And how did she keep reenacting his fantasies?

Now was not the time to drool and wonder if she'd do a strip tease and actually fire the weapon—and he didn't mean the one in her hands. Something had his vixen agitated. In seconds, Boris had exited his truck and bolted the dozen yards separating them.

"Did you see him?" Jan asked, peeking around his broad frame.

"See who? What the fuck is going on? Get your damp ass back in your house before you turn into an icicle." Because already the wet blonde wisps escaping the towel turban on her head froze in the cool air and her moist skin pebbled.

"Some guard you are," she huffed as she whirled without further explanation and stalked back inside. He followed, shutting the door behind him. Yet an explanation wasn't forthcoming. Gun still in hand, she headed to the sliding patio door at the rear of her townhouse. Curious, he shadowed her.

"Care to explain what you are talking about? What the hell's got you so spooked?"

"I am not spooked. I am annoyed. Learn to know the difference," she snapped as she yanked the curtain open and flipped a switch, illuminating her tiny yard. She peered out the rear window, but other than a few bunny tracks— brave little suckers considering the predators living on this block—nothing marred the pristine surface of the snow.

"Annoyed about what? And would you please explain why you're toting a gun around?"

"For defense of course. Someone was in my house."

Boris almost stumbled on the stairs where he followed her delectable ass, barely covered in her towel. An ass he was pretty sure was bare underneath. Drool.

Her words penetrated. "What do you mean someone was in your house? I inspected the place. No one was here." Or had she addled him to the extent that, once again, he'd missed an obvious clue?

"Whoever it was came in while I was showering and left me another note. On my bed."

His heart stuttered to a stop, probably because his blood turned to ice. Surely he'd misunderstood. "Say that again."

"How much clearer would you like me to be? Someone left me a note while I was naked in the shower," she growled as she stomped into the bedroom he'd inspected earlier.

He wanted to deny her claim, explain it away and say they must have missed it, but then he walked into the bedroom. The distinct scent of another hung in the air. Not just another. A bear. A polar bear. *Gene.*

Gene was here.

But how? The backdoor showed no signs of entry. The front he would have seen.

And there was no way he'd missed the polar bear's presence during his sweep. *Even I'm not that dim-witted.*

"Let me see the note."

"It's on the bed." She waved her gun-toting hand in its direction as she wandered to an open door, which, judging by the clothes hanging within, was a closet.

Boris snatched the missive and read.

Peek-a-boo, I see you. And might I say, you're looking foxy. I can't wait to make you mine. Signed once again, *Your Ghostly admirer.*

"Still going to tell me it's the asshole who works in the mine?" he rumbled, crumpling the missive and tossing it. Given it didn't go far, break anything or hit anyone, it didn't do much to alleviate his fear-driven rage.

"Okay, so maybe you're right. I have a stalker. Maybe even this Gene guy who's got it out for Reid."

"Reid and possibly anyone else he served with."

"But I was never in the army. I never even met the man, so why me? Why now?"

He knew why, because Gene obviously included Boris in the group of people he blamed for his torture at the hands of their captors. But he didn't say it aloud. Boris didn't like to talk about that time. Somehow, Gene mistakenly thought Jan meant something to him. Okay, maybe not quite mistaken, he did care for her. As a friend. A friend he wanted to see naked. Grrr.

"Who the fuck knows why?" he snapped. "The bear's obviously deranged. A better question is, how did he get in?"

"Attic," she answered from the depths of her closet.

"How do you know that?" he asked, moving to find her, only to stop dead at the sight of her bare legs dangling from a hatch in the ceiling inside the closet.

And yup, his earlier guess of her wearing no panties? Totally on the mark. But he ignored her pink perfection to focus on the more important thing at hand. "Get your fucking ass down from there, woman. What are you, stupid?"

"I'll come when I'm ready."

Or when he pleasured her. Bad thought. He averted his gaze from the source of the naughty ideas. "Get down here before I paddle your dumb," —yet so utterly sweet—"ass."

"Don't call me names, Boris Sobolev."

Down she hopped into his arms, which he thrust out at the last moment, snagging her. Her tucked towel still clung to her body but did little to hide her curves. He ignored her delectable frame in favor of his irritation. "I'll call you whatever I like when you act rashly. Again."

"I was following my nose."

"Right into trouble."

"There's no one up there."

"Now. What if he'd still been hiding in the attic? He could have killed you. Or grabbed you as hostage." Or touched the bare skin exposed by her flimsy towel.

"Well, he wasn't. However, I did learn an interesting fact. The attics for these townhouses are all interconnected. He probably went in through the end unit that's for sale and then counted hatches before paying mine a visit. A better question is why? What was he hoping to accomplish? I'm more annoyed than afraid."

Funny, because Boris was feeling quite the opposite. Gene had set out to rattle him and to show him how easily he could get to Jan. How the bear had figured out she was his weak spot, Boris didn't know, but he did understand all too well the art of mind warfare. Thus far, Gene was winning.

"Pack a bag."

"What for?"

"Because you're not staying here." The townhouse wasn't secure.

"I'm not going anywhere."

"Yes, you are, before Gene comes back."

"Don't be silly. This Gene guy hasn't done anything to hurt me."

"Yet. You might not be so lucky next time."

"And exactly where do you expect me to go?"

"My place."

She blinked at him. "Say that again?"

"I said you can come stay at my place."

The sweet tinkling sound of her laughter surrounded him. "Oh, Boris. You are so funny. As if I'm going to move in with you."

"I see nothing amusing about it."

Her lips curved into a smile. "You know, if you want us to live together, and share a bed, you just need to say so."

Wake up to her gorgeous face each morning? Her body cradled into his? Her scream of fright as, in his nightmare, he held a gun to her head and tried to kill her? "I am not asking you to marry me. I'm offering my home as a haven to keep you safe."

Like a cloud passing in front of the sun, her brilliant smile disappeared. "Perish the thought of us hooking up. Thanks for the offer, but no thanks. I'll take my chances here."

"But the attic—"

"Can be nailed shut. I sleep with a gun under my pillow. I'll make sure I have one by the tub when I bathe," *—oh god, her naked with a weapon!—* "and if Gene shows up, I'll give your regards before I shoot him dead. Unless he's really cute and means what he says. Then maybe I'll run away with him and we can start a new life."

He couldn't help his roar. Yes, moose could roar if agitated enough, and by damn did Jan ever manage to do that with ease. "You will stop with your jokes. This is not funny, Jan. You are leaving with me."

"No. Now, if you don't mind, I'd like to get dressed. This wet towel is getting mighty uncomfortable."

And then she did it. The one thing guaranteed to addle what wits remained to him. She dropped the towel. Bared it all. Turned away from him, presenting her bare backside so she could thumb through her rack of clothes.

A man could only take so much.

He could also take what was right before him.

With her hair bound up in a towel, he had no problem rubbing the rasp of his chin against the tender skin of her neck as his hands gripped her around the slim indent of her waist. He ground his groin, the fabric of his jeans an irritating barrier, against the rounded cheeks of her buttocks.

She gasped, but didn't fight to escape his grasp. Even when he growled against her skin, "You're driving me even further into insanity, woman."

"And I've been crazy for you since the moment we met. Your point would be?"

He nipped at her flesh, a shudder running through him at her moan of pleasure. "I'm not the man for you."

"You're the only man for me." She turned in his grasp, her delicate hands reaching to cup his unshaven jaw. "Let me in."

Before he could say, "I can't," she kissed him.

Where the insurgents might have lacked the skill to break him, Jan, sweet, fucking Jan, demolished him, and in that moment, he gave her what she wanted. He gave her himself.

Actually, he didn't give, more like took. Because, dammit, he was the man, and he'd waited a damned long time for this moment.

He plundered the warm recess of her mouth, his tongue sweeping in and laying claim to hers. He ran it along the sharp edge of her teeth. Tasted her. Imprinted her flavor so he would never forget.

As if he could ever forget Jan. The woman owned a part of his heart, maybe even his soul, despite his attempts to keep her out.

But he wasn't worried about that at this moment. No, he was more concerned with how to shed his clothing so he could press her delectable body against his. Skin to skin.

Hoisting her slight frame, he walked them out of the closet, and he laid her on her bed, his lips never once losing contact as his hands practically popped the buttons on his shirt in his haste to shed it. He had an irritating moment where he wobbled as he tried to step out of his jeans, which he'd unbuttoned and shoved down. However, he managed to kick them away without losing his balance and crushing her.

Lips still locked, he knelt on the bed, the mattress dipping with his weight. Her hands rubbed the length of his biceps, stroking him, a simple touch, but even something so small was enough to turn his breath ragged. Sparing one hand, he used it to grasp her roaming fingers and then pinned her wrists above her head. With one arm only, he held himself over her, the magnetic sizzle of her bared skin tempting him to lower himself.

Not yet.

Despite the sweetness of her lips, he nonetheless tore his mouth away, determined to see to her pleasure first before he completely lost it. He'd never felt so out of control, so needy, so aroused.

Her creamy white skin beckoned. Bending forward, he placed his mouth on her neck, the flutter of her pulse erratic, just like her heartbeat. His mouth slid down and hit the swell of her breast. Jan squirmed, but he held her down, so whilst her lower body undulated, and for a brief moment made contact with his bared flesh, he held back from giving her what her moans demanded.

I will make you come first.

The puckered tip of her breast met the warmth of his mouth, and she cried out. He would have smiled, but he was too busy suckling the nipple, drawing it into his mouth and fulfilling one of his many fantasies. He swapped to the other one, lavishing upon it the same attention, enjoying her low moans and smelling her arousal.

Oh, I have to taste. Despite the luscious pleasure of her nipples, he traveled downward, over her flat belly to the almost white curls covering her mound. He nuzzled her, and her hips twitched. He rubbed his cheek against the softness of her upper thigh, the tremor of her limb bringing a smile to his lips. He placed a soft kiss on first one then the other thigh before he pressed his face against her pubes, inhaling her sweet scent.

He could hold out no longer.

He steadied her with his hands, loving the leanness of her body and her wanton reactions to his touch. Using his lips only, he grazed the petals of her sex.

Oh how she bucked, and mewled, and squirmed.

Again, he brushed his mouth against her, licking his lips and groaning as her honey hit his taste buds.

He now better understood why bears didn't like to divvy up their sweet treats. Between Jan's thighs, he found a treasure he never wanted to share. *Mine. All mine.* Need, possessive need took hold of him. He let his mouth devour her, basking in Jan's ambrosia, determined to make her scream his name. *Mine.*

With her legs spread and her pink sex exposed to him, he lapped at her moist core, and oh, how she bucked. Distracted and losing his latch once, or twice, he flattened his palms against her and held her still. With one outlet taken away, she relieved some of her tension by weaving fingers into his short hair, tugging him closer.

Fuck, but she tasted sweet, and addictive, better than anything he'd ever known. As for her scent, her arousal, her need for him? That drove him absolutely wild.

Over and over, he lapped at her, paying special attention to her sensitive nub, enjoying her keening cries. His touch made her slick and hot. He shoved two fingers into her channel and was unable to stop a groan at the tight feel of her clamping around him.

"Fuck me. You are so fucking tight and perfect." She didn't reply, unless her drawn-out scream counted as he triggered a climax with his thrusting fingers.

Wild and at the edge himself, he needed to feel her around him, now. As his fingers pumped her still quivering channel, he positioned himself, the head of his cock thick and ready. He pressed his thumb against her swollen button, and she moaned loudly as her head thrashed on the pillow.

"Boris." She said his name like a breathy plea.

His name.

Mine.

He could wait no longer. He guided himself into her sex, sinking into her welcoming heat, inch by inch, his muscles tensing as he fought to go slow. Her sex stretched to accommodate him, a tight fist which he longed to pound, but he held back.

Jan was petite. Fragile. Perfect. And … begging him to stop torturing her?

"Take me, Boris. Please. I can't take anymore."

He slammed his cock home. Or should he say into heaven? It surely felt like blissful perfection, all that heat, moisture, and the quivering of her channel welcoming him.

He might have stayed balls deep in her forever if she'd not wiggled her hips and said, "Move it, moose. I'm not going to break."

Past words, he could only grunt as he began to seesaw back and forth, thrusting in and out, adopting a fast, rhythmic cadence that she matched. Their bodies rocked in harmony. Their hearts pounded erratically. Their lips locked, and they shared one breath as they rocketed to pleasure.

When her second climax rippled through her, he was right there with her, his cock jerking wildly within her, her sex milking him and drawing out his ecstasy.

He groaned her name, and she whispered his, the moment unbelievably intimate and perfect.

Despite feeling drained, he remembered himself enough to not collapse on her and crush her beneath his greater weight. But he didn't go far. Lying alongside her in bed, he couldn't help but cradle her in his arms, her cheek pressed to his chest, the top of her silky head just under his chin. Their legs ended up intertwined.

Not a word was spoken. Anything said now would have surely broken the magical moment. For once, Boris didn't want to think or do the right thing, or even move.

Just let me have a few minutes of peace. Perfection. Let me have one memory of what my life could have been like.

Before he knew it, they'd fallen asleep.

Chapter Ten

It started with him mumbling. "No. No." A lowly chanted denial to go with the roll of his head on the pillow.

Someone's having a nightmare. Woken by his motions, Jan leaned on an elbow and peered at Boris, his features illuminated by the green digital glow of her alarm clock. Poor guy, his expression was anything but relaxed. Brow furrowed and his lips tight, he thrashed, his movement getting more and more wild.

Reaching out a hand, she placed it on his cheek, meaning to soothe him. "It's okay, Boris. You're having a—" Squeak.

Finishing her sentence proved impossible as he rolled atop her, one hand at her throat squeezing while he continued to mumble, louder now, "No! Fuck you. I won't say nothing. I'll kill you first."

Definitely a possibility given Jan's predicament. While a more docile female might have let her lover choke her to death. Jan wasn't that woman. Problem was, how to stop him?

Given his size and obvious lack of ability to discern whom he choked, she doubted she could pry his fingers off or wrestle him away. She could grab at the gun she kept close by, but shooting Boris seemed a touch extreme. But she did have one weapon in her arsenal that would do no lasting damage and was sure to wake him.

With her vision polka dotting from lack of oxygen, she said a mental sorry and kneed him in the jewels.

He drew in a breath, a big one, and his grip on her neck loosened, enough that she could holler, "Boris, wake up!"

Instantly, his eyes popped open and his body went still. He gazed down upon her then lower at the hand still circling her neck. Horror filled his eyes.

She couldn't miss the anguish in his whispered, "Fuck me, what have I done?"

Lightning quick, he rolled off her and kept going until he stood beside the bed, every muscle in his body taut with agitation. He paced the side of her bed as he mumbled, "Fuck. I'm so sorry. Fuck. I should have known better. Fuck. Fuck. FUCK!" His last expletive exploded a millisecond before his fist hit the wall, her poor plaster wall, which now sported a big hole.

Boris cursed again and resumed pacing, mumbling under his breath. Jan pulled herself into a seated position against her headboard and watched him. When he seemed done with his mini tantrum, or so she assumed because his shoulders slumped, she said, "Are you done cussing and wrecking the joint?"

A chagrined moose with a hanging head wouldn't meet her eyes. "I'm sorry."

This wouldn't do at all, not after the way they'd finally connected. Some would have called it sex, but Jan knew what happened was something more. Their joining was the start. Or would have been. Already she could sense him pulling away, regretting what they'd done.

She tried to lighten the mood. "You will be sorry because I not only expect you to patch that hole, but given color matching rarely works, you've now volunteered yourself to paint the whole bedroom too."

Up snapped his head, and he met her gaze, eyes ablaze with anger, and misery. His voice emerged gruff with emotion. "That's all you're worried about? Making sure I fix the damage? Who the fuck cares about a measly fucking hole? I just tried to choke you in my sleep."

"You were having a nightmare." She shrugged. "It happens."

"Yeah, it happens, every goddamned night. It's why I don't sleep with people. It's why I tried to stay away from you. It's why I didn't want this to happen." He gestured to the rumpled bed, which still smelled of sex.

Oh no, he was not going to use this as an excuse. He wasn't the only one to blame. "I should have known better than to touch you while you were having a nightmare. Next time, I'll try talking to you first."

He raked a hand over his short hair. "Next time? There won't be a fucking next time. I warned you I was damaged. I'm not safe for you to be around."

She snorted. "You're not safe? Um, did you miss the part where I woke you by kneeing you in your manparts? I'd say if anyone was in real danger it was you. Lucky for you, I was awake and knew it was you, else you might have woken to a gun in the face."

His jaw dropped. "You have a gun in here."

"I told you before, I keep one under my pillow."

"Loaded?"

She couldn't help a roll of her eyes. "Of course it's loaded. It wouldn't do me much good empty, now would it?"

He scrubbed his face, and as he once again paced, he mumbled some more. "Oh fuck, that could have been so bad. Oh fuck." His self-recrimination she could handle. But him getting dressed and hiding that delectable body? No way.

"Where do you think you're going?" she demanded.

"I need to leave."

"It's the middle of the night. Come back to bed. We need to talk about this."

"There is nothing to say, Jan."

"I'd say there's plenty. Starting with why you have these nightmares and what can we do to stop them."

"It's part of my post-traumatic stress shit, or so the fucking military shrink said. And no, I don't want to talk about it. I just want to forget it. But I can't. Drugs. Alcohol. Big fucking joints. It doesn't matter what they give me, or I try, there's nothing that stops them. I've tried. Tried so fucking hard."

"Yeah, but before you didn't have me to help you."

"Exactly. Which meant I couldn't hurt you, hence why I have to leave."

He meant it. Traumatized by what he'd almost done, he would go. Thing was, could she ever get him to return? "What about what happened here? We made love, Boris. Doesn't that count for something?"

Pain flashed across his features, quickly followed by cold resolve.

Her stomach tightened.

"I warned you I wasn't the man for you. What happened tonight hasn't changed that."

Oh, but it had. Before, Jan could still hope that maybe she could forget Boris. Now, however, she'd gotten a taste of the passion and the caring she could have in his arms. No way could she settle for anyone else. Unfortunately, he seemed determined. "So what, you're just going to walk out?" She couldn't help the angry lilt to her words. She thought she'd finally gotten through to him. Shown him how good they could be together. And they were *good*. Her pleasantly sore body could attest to that, and yet there he was, ready to leave.

"It's safer for you this way."

"Safer for you, you mean. I've said it before, and I'll say it again. You're a great big chicken, Boris."

"I'm a menace."

"Only when you sleep. We can deal with it. I can use a separate bedroom. Or we could handcuff you to the bed. Which might be a lot of fun actually, now that I think of it." Mmm, just thinking of the possibilities of a tethered Boris, naked and at her mercy, made her wet.

He, on the other hand, didn't seem as intrigued given his jean-clad butt was headed out the door.

"Don't you dare leave!" she yelled.

He didn't reply.

So she played dirty. "What if Gene comes back? We never did nail that attic shut. Are you just going to leave me here, alone? Defenseless?" Okay, so she exaggerated. She'd blow the head off any intruder who dared to accost her. However, she hoped her words would ignite Boris' instinct to protect. "I thought you were supposed to keep me safe?" Oh, how her daddy would have howled to hear her false plea. It worked, though.

The tread of his feet on the stairs paused. He uttered a loud sigh. She held her breath and waited.

Slowly, he returned, not meeting her gaze, shoulders slumped in defeat. He didn't come back to bed, though. Nope. He went straight to her closet and threw himself on the carpeted floor, the tips of his feet hanging out the doorway.

He wasn't seriously planning on sleeping there, was he?

Given he didn't move or say a word, she could only surmise he was. For a moment, she debated ordering him back to bed, but given how close he'd come to leaving, she let the not quite sleeping man lie.

One step at a time.

Her moose wasn't kidding when he said he had issues. They would take more than one night of sex or words to fix. Lucky for him, she'd inherited her mother and father's tenacious nature. Boris might try and go back to the way things were, but now that Jan had wiggled through a crack in his armored heart, no way was he keeping her out.

I'm here to stay, even if I have to outfox you into becoming a permanent part of my life.

Chapter Eleven

Sleep eluded Boris and not because he lay upon the floor of a closet. He'd slept in worse spots. Cushy carpet sure beat hard-packed dirt any day.

Slumber didn't pass him by because he worried about an incursion by Gene—*bring it*—or because he feared a recurrence of the nightmare. Lie. His fear he might harm her in his sleep might have played a small part. No guy liked waking up choking the woman he'd just bedded, especially when the sex was amazing.

Nope, the real reason he couldn't slip into repose was because Jan rested less than a dozen feet from him. Only nine if he measured by his own clodhoppers. It would take but the barest moment for him to slip back into that warm bed with her. A bed that smelled of Jan and sex. Wonderful sex. Awesome sex. Fucking amazing, goddamn-it-all-he-wanted-it-again sex.

He clenched his fists, lest he punch something else of hers and she demand he replace her wardrobe. He still couldn't believe the balls of her, telling him after he'd almost throttled her to death that he'd have to patch and paint her room.

Did she not grasp the severity of what he'd almost done?

Why did she not show any fear? *Handcuff me indeed.* She'd meant it as a safety measure, but all he could think of was how he'd love to have his body at her tender, and passionate, mercy.

I am a sick bastard. Sick and stupid and way too emotionally involved with Jan despite his vow to not get close.

So much for keeping his distance. If he'd thought her hard to resist before, how the fuck would he cope now he knew what a vixen she was in bed?

Turned out she was also just as snuggly on the floor.

"What the hell do you think you're doing?" he growled as she crawled into the closet and draped herself atop him, her silky body still naked.

"Cuddling. It's a thing people do."

Other people. Not him. "I don't cuddle."

As if she listened. She snuggled her face into the T-shirt covering his chest. "You are now."

"You need to get some sleep."

"I will if you stop talking."

"In your bed."

"I'm fine where I am."

He couldn't help the rumbling growl. "You are frustrating me."

"Welcome to the club. Although mine has more to do with the sexual kind. Care to fix it?" She wiggled against him, and his already semi-erect cock expanded to press against her body in a way she couldn't miss.

"I thought I told you to leave me alone."

"You said a lot of things. Most of it I didn't pay attention to. Given you were determined to beat yourself up, I thought about letting you stew in your misery."

"But?" Because he could tell she was holding back.

She giggled. Seriously, she fucking giggled before she said, "But I hear misery loves company. So here I am."

"Your cuteness isn't going to work," he growled. What a lie. Already his tension was easing. Well, the stress kind at least. The tension below his belt? Yeah, that wasn't leaving until he either slapped it silly or gave her what she wanted.

"Aha, you do think I'm cute." She sounded inordinately pleased.

"As if you didn't know that. Cuteness won't save you, though, if I accidentally fall asleep and have one of my nightmares again."

"So we don't sleep. I can think of better things to do."

Again, she wiggled, and he couldn't help the groan that slipped from him.

"Why must you make this so hard?"

"Well, it wouldn't be any fun if it was soft."

It took him a half second to grasp her dirty innuendo. Jan. Talking dirty. To him.

A surge of lust went through him, which wasn't surprising. It was the laughter shaking his frame that really shocked him the most. He chuckled, and it seemed the sound stunned her because she went still before joining him.

When their mirth ended, she cupped his face, her hands soft and her gaze gentle. "You know, that's probably the first time I've heard you laugh since you came back."

"Not quite the first, but I've not found much to amuse me these past few years."

"How did it feel?"

He frowned, but before he could ask what she meant, she elucidated. "How did it feel to just let go?"

The question stumped him for a moment because the answer was unexpected. *It felt good.* Which couldn't be right.

A cold beer after a hard day felt good going down. A good night's sleep, without the nightmares—courtesy of sleeping pills he didn't like—felt good because he woke refreshed. Sex, with Jan, felt fucking great. And laughing with his fox because she was just being herself and spending time with him? It felt good. More than that, it felt natural. Normal. Wonderful.

And when was the last time he could claim that?

Before he could tell her, a subtle creak from above caught his attention. Possibly the townhouse settling. Or a mouse scampering. Or any number of normal things.

What wasn't normal was the curl of smoke that seeped from the crack where the trap door to the attic was shut, but not sealed air-tight.

"Fire."

She wrinkled her brow. "How is that a feeling?"

He answered her as he wrapped an arm around her waist and sat, dragging her with him. "Someone just lit a fire in your attic."

"I think you mean a little lower."

What a dirty-minded vixen. Any other time he would have appreciated it. "No, your attic, as in up there." He pointed.

"What?" Her wide eyes glanced at the ceiling, where the thin miasma of smoke was starting to spread.

She scrambled to her feet and screeched. Again, not a maidenly cry of distress, but of rage. "Oh you've got to be kidding. First, my truck gets written off because some fiends shot at it, and now someone has set fire to my townhouse! When I get my hands on the culprit, I'm going to tie him to a stretching rack and skin him alive."

It might have been a more effective threat if she'd not hollered it while naked with her hands planted on her hips. As it was, Boris found it more arousing than threatening. But Jan appearing gorgeous or not, he couldn't allow himself to get distracted, not with the smoke thickening.

"Get dressed, quickly. We need to leave before this fire spreads too far."

As she rapidly donned some garments and filled a bag, the crackle of the flames became evident and the fire alarm outside her bedroom in the hall began its ear piercing shriek.

Boris had called the fire department on his cell phone while she readied herself. In the distance, he could already hear the shrill sirens.

As Jan skipped down the stairs, Boris on her heels, she tossed him a glance over her shoulder. "We need to make sure everyone is getting out."

"I'll handle it once we get outside and you've scampered to safety."

She opened her mouth, probably to argue, but before she could utter a word, the big bay window in her living room suddenly shattered, and something went whizzing by his head.

What the fuck?

"Did someone just shoot at us?" Jan asked.

Someone sure had. "Get down," he ordered.

An unnecessary command given she'd already dropped to the ground and slithered to the broken window, which let in cold blasts of air. The appearance of a pistol in her hand no longer had the capacity to surprise him. His fox had many layers to her, each more fascinating than the last.

Of course, he didn't heed his own advice about ducking and the next shot sliced across the skin of his bicep. It stung, but it pissed him off more than anything.

You want to play with ammo and fire? Then let's play.

Jan and their unseen assailant weren't the only ones with a gun. He pulled his out of his coat pocket, which still lay on the floor where he'd dropped it when he'd followed Jan back into her house. But before he used it, he placed it on the floor beside him as he ducked down to put on his boots. Bare feet and ice did not go well together. He did, however, leave them loosely laced so he could kick them off quickly if he needed to shift.

"Stay here and stay down," he told her as he put his hand on the knob to the front door.

Ducked below the picture window frame, she turned her head to look at him. "What do you think you're doing?" she hissed. "If you go out there, you'll be making yourself into a giant target."

Her point? "How else am I supposed to catch the asshole taking potshots?" And get her out of her burning house safely?

"We could wait until help arrives. It will probably scare him off."

Women and their logic. He snorted and opened the door, holding in a grunt of pain as a bullet hit him in the thigh. Lucky for him, the shooter had shitty aim. Less lucky for him, he'd probably hear an earful about not listening from Jan when she noticed.

Out on the street, there wasn't a creature stirring—except for a moose. Gun in one hand, and limping, Boris ducked behind a porch support, which offered scant shielding but made him into a smaller target. Peering around the edge, he couldn't see a thing in the gloom. But he was only a few feet from Jan's neighbor. He dove out of hiding and jammed his finger on the doorbell, making it go off in a shrill series of ding-dongs.

A crack sounded, but no new flare of pain accompanied it, so he did his best to make himself less of a target behind the neighbor's porch post and took a moment to listen before again diving out and hitting the next doorbell. He needn't have bothered, the door flung open as soon as he began, and a bedraggled older couple, in their nightclothes—and her wearing a cap over her curlers—came rushing out.

Before he could tell them to take cover, the one fire truck in town arrived and pandemonium ensued. The good news was, if you discounted his bullet wound, no one got hurt, the bad news? The roof on the townhouse units collapsed, and someone got to the gunman before him.

Even more disturbing. The body they found wasn't Gene. As a matter of fact, the guy who'd taken potshots at them wasn't anyone they knew.

However, before he could mull over what this meant, Jan caught the scent or sight of his bleeding leg, and all hell broke loose.

Chapter Twelve

A few moments before Jan got violent with a stubborn moose...

Gene cuffed the idiot with the gun, sending him flying just as he was about to take another cowardly shot.

"What the fuck do you think you're doing?" Gene snarled.

The seal pup, a young man in his twenties, who should have never left the ocean, didn't raise a hand to defend himself but remained lying on his back. Cowardly bunch the seals, soft not just in appearance but character.

As far as Gene was concerned, the only good seal was one basted in herbs and slow roasted over a campfire. Not the sentient kind of course, unless they were real annoying. Those ones tasted better sushi-style raw. Nothing like slicing off a blubbery chunk from a belligerent bull to get him and his buddies waddling back to the ocean they came from. Encroach on his territory indeed. This polar bear didn't like to share.

"I was just following orders," whined the seal, whom Gene recognized because he'd seen him around back at the main camp. A camp that kept moving and which he'd not returned to in a while not liking the direction things were going.

"Whose orders?" Gene growled. Certainly not his. He'd opted to work alone in his quest to torment those who'd left him behind.

"*He* told me to."

He, as in the scary dude who'd found Gene in the cesspool overseas he'd called home for a while after he escaped the insurgents prison. Damaged in mind, spirit, and body, Gene had wallowed a while in liquor and misery, until *He* gave him purpose again and set him on his path to vengeance.

A vengeance he thought they'd agreed upon. Apparently not. *We'll be having words about that.*

This wasn't the first time Gene had to step in and cull some anxious recruits who overstepped their bounds. He'd taken out from afar another who'd almost spilled his guts to Reid when captured.

And now, this pup thought to disrupt his carefully cultivated plot.

"This town is mine," Gene rumbled as he grasped the pup's collar and hauled him to his feet.

"You're taking too long. He needs the towns catering to shifters, like Kodiak Point and the rest, to fold sooner."

"Why?" What had happened to make him want to speed up their timeframe? That wasn't part of the plan. In order to fully take over the clan, Gene needed to weaken the current alpha. To cultivate an atmosphere of uncertainty and fear. Then, when Reid and his merry band were taken out, Gene could step in and take over.

At least that was his plan. It seemed his freaky benefactor was stirring more than one pot. Not for long.

"Does it matter why he wants this town?" asked the belligerent pup. "He just does. And I do as I'm told. So should you if you know what's good for you. He's not going to be happy when he finds out you stopped me from fulfilling my orders."

"Lucky for me, he won't be finding out." Gene tossed the irritating seal over the lip of the roof they stood on. Extreme, but effective. He leaned over the edge to see the little fucker had absorbed some of the fall with his fat. The stubborn bugger rolled to his knees with a grunt. He couldn't have the annoying bastard tattle telling, so Gene put a bullet in him.

Dead men couldn't talk. And dead men couldn't ruin his plans for vengeance.

Because Gene wasn't done playing with Boris yet.

Chapter Thirteen

It took Jan a while to corner her moose, and when she finally did, he and a grim-faced Reid stood over the body of a stranger splayed in an alley between two duplexes, a short distance from her place.

"Who is he?" she asked as she tucked herself into Boris' side, a pleased grin curling her lips when his arm stretched around her, automatically hugging her into his body. "Is it your old army buddy, Gene?"

"Nope, but it looks like we found our shooter," Reid replied.

"And you didn't keep him alive for questioning?" It came out a tad plaintive because Jan sure wanted to know the answer as to why the jerk felt a need to take potshots after torching her place. She was also miffed someone robbed her of a chance to poke him with a sharp stick and smack him around a few times for destroying her home.

"Trust me, we would have preferred him kicking and screaming."

"Definitely screaming," Boris agreed with a grunt.

"But someone didn't want him to talk. He was dead when we found him. From the looks of it, he was shoved off the roof and then someone put a bullet in him to make sure he didn't get up and walk away."

"Thorough," she remarked.

"That's Gene for you," Reid replied.

The alpha for the clan, and her boss at Beark Enterprises, didn't appear too angry at the situation, more tired and resigned. Sometimes being head honcho, especially over a rabble of wild animals who, if left in their natural habitat, would never get along, made for some tough decisions and irritating situations. But Reid had the broad shoulders to handle it—and a don't-screw-with-me attitude.

At six-foot-something, he stood only slightly shorter than Boris, but he was huge, his Kodiak bear gene accounting for much of his muscle mass. Jan had known him since she was a kid, having hung out with his sister—who'd moved to Anchorage years ago for a taste of the city life. Jan at times wished she'd followed, especially when Boris spent so many years pretending she didn't exist.

Of course, it seemed her waiting had paid off. She couldn't help but smile again as she tucked her arm around his waist, enjoying the solid feel of him, the tingle of awareness. She even loved his scent, a mixture of man and strong soap, none of that cloying cologne spray for her moose. She breathed in deep and frowned because the odor of fresh blood tickled her nose, odd given the body on the ground had stopped oozing a while ago, the cold temperatures freezing the liquid seeping from the perfectly round wound in his head.

Was someone injured? Reid had arrived after the fire trucks and missed the gun play, but Boris ... Boris had lumbered right out into the open. Surely he would have said something if hit? Boris, admit something? As if.

She slid out from under his arm and pivoted to check him over. She immediately saw his bloody thigh. His freshly bleeding thigh.

Her gaze rose to meet his nonchalant one. She arched a brow. "You're hit."

"Yup."

Her lips thinned. "And yet, you're standing around here yapping instead of getting it treated."

"I tried to get him to see a medic," Reid said.

"You didn't try hard enough," she snapped to her boss.

"He's a grown man. I figured it was his choice."

"He's an idiot."

"Who's standing right here," Boris grumbled.

"Which is even more idiotic. That bullet is still in there. Exactly how do you expect to heal properly if we don't get it out? Not to mention the fact the longer it stays in, the more damage we'll have to inflict pulling it out." Because shifters healed rapidly, which meant they'd have to reopen the wound to remove the bullet.

His expression turned sheepish. "I was going to take care of it once I knew the gunman was caught."

"He's dead, and you will be too if you don't march your butt over to the clinic and get that fixed right now, Boris Sobolev."

Chagrin turned to stubborn mutiny. "You can't tell me what to do."

Challenge her, would he? She straightened her spine and met his gaze without backing down.

"Um, Boris," Reid tried to interject in a low voice. "You might want to—"

Jan cut Reid off with a glare. Her boss might be alpha of the clan and a big freaking bear, but even he knew better than to come between a vixen and her mate. Almost mate, but close enough. Now that they'd become intimate, whether he was ready to accept it or not, Boris was hers. And as her male, he would take care of himself or face her wrath.

"Are you seriously going to argue with me about going to see the doctor?" she asked in a sweet voice, because Momma always taught her you catch more flies with honey. Or was it trapped more bears? In her case, she needed to net a moose. Where was the family shotgun when a vixen needed it?

"I'll go see him when I'm damned well ready. I've got stuff to do and..." His words tapered off, probably because of the handgun she held aimed at him. "What the hell, woman?"

Her momma also said men were idiots and often prone to doing moronic things because of testosterone, which meant it was up to women to take care of them when stupidity overtook their brains. "Get your sweet buttocks moving, or so help me, Boris, I will put a hole in your other leg and drag you there myself."

"You wouldn't dare."

Reid cleared his throat. "Um, I wouldn't challenge her on this. She once shot Johnny in the ass with buckshot when his mom ended up in the clinic and he wouldn't go to visit her."

"You did not."

"I did." Jan shrugged. "His poor sick mother was so happy to see him, even if he was flat on his belly getting pellets plucked out of his cheeks."

"But I can't leave now. Reid needs me."

With a shake of his head, Reid distanced himself from the brewing battle. "Oh no you don't. You are not using me to get out of this one, dude. I might rule this clan, but I swear, Jan's taken lessons from my Aunt Betty-Sue."

The two males shuddered. Betty-Sue was known for keeping boys in line, a trait Jan's own mother much admired, hence the tips she'd gleaned from her friend and imparted on Jan, her daughter.

The threat had the desired effect, though. With a mumble about bossy vixens, Boris let her lead him away, his slight limp not softening her in the least but actually firing her irritation as just another sign of his stubbornness when it came to his own well-being.

"What if the doc's not answering when we get there?" he asked as he stuffed himself in her little loaner of a car, which she'd borrowed from a friend who preferred to use their snowmobile this time of the year.

"She lives right next door. Which you well know. She'll be around."

"I would have taken myself you know. You didn't have to threaten me."

"Someone's got to take care of you seeing as how you seem incapable of caring for yourself."

"I've been doing fine so far."

"Says the guy who has nightmares and would prefer to sleep in a closet than with me."

"That was a low blow."

"It was. I'm sorry."

Her apology took him aback. "Did you just say sorry?"

"I'll have you know I'm capable of admitting when I'm wrong, unlike a certain moosehead I know."

"I'm not wrong. And tonight proved it in spades. Because of me, you were almost killed. First at my hands, then by a fire set to trap me, and then by gunfire, again, meant to take me out.

"The first isn't your fault and we can work on it. As for the other two…" She tossed her hair over her shoulder and shot him a mischievous look. "How do you know it's not my secret admirer lashing out because I dared cheat on him with another man?"

"I thought we'd ascertained Gene was behind those stalking notes."

"No. You assumed he was. I just agreed he might be. Is it so far-fetched for you to imagine that, in spying on Reid, my shy stalker fell for the lovely and efficient secretary and when he saw you debauching my lovely, nubile body he had a jealous fit?"

Boris snorted. "That's the biggest load of crap I've ever heard. You been reading too many romance novels if you ask me."

"You are such a jerk."

"What did I do now?" He seemed genuinely puzzled, so she clued him in.

"Is it so hard to believe that I might have the ability to inspire jealousy? Or are you going to tell me that if the roles were reversed, and you saw me making out with another guy, you'd be fine with it?"

"What other guy?" he growled.

"Doesn't matter. Would it bother you?"

"No," he spat through gritted teeth. "Because we are not involved."

"Wow, you are in utter denial."

"No, I'm doing what I have to in order to keep you safe. If Gene is after me, then anyone involved with me is in danger."

"But if you don't care about me, then why do you give a hoof if I'm targeted?"

"I never said I didn't care."

"Aha, so you do like me."

"Of course, I do. As a friend."

Her turn to growl.

"A good friend?"

She slammed a fist down on his injured thigh, and he yelled. Good. Tit for tat. Pain for pain.

"What do you want me to say?"

"I want you to admit what we have is special and stop pretending it isn't."

"But I don't want to."

She would have hit him again, but he grabbed her fist, wrapping his fingers around it. "Enough. You can't beat me on this point. Physically or mentally."

He was right. She couldn't force him to love her. Besides, what happened to playing aloof and making him chase her? *But I thought with our sleeping together that...* What? Boris would suddenly turn into an ardent lover and mate? That her love would cure all his problems at once?

She was the idiot, not him.

The rest of the drive passed in silence, and she pulled into the clinic just as lights flickered in the main office window. It seemed someone, probably Reid, had called ahead and warned of their impending arrival.

Boris got out and slammed the door shut. He'd made it a few steps to the clinic before he realized she didn't follow. He turned, a frown on his face, but Jan ignored it and, with a wave, backed out.

Right now she was too emotionally charged to be in the same room with him. She needed some distance and maybe a second perspective. *I also need a new plan of attack.*

And some fresh cookies with milk. With Momma in Florida basking in the sun, there was only one person she knew who could whip up a batch and dispense advice.

Less than half an hour later, with dawn cresting, not that you could tell by the thick darkness, she sat on a stool in Reid's kitchen while his grandmother, Ursula—everyone called her Ursa, which meant mother bear—mixed together the ingredients for chocolate chip cookies.

Even better, Jan had the company of her new best friend, Tammy, the alpha's mate, a city girl recently turned shifter who could offer a fresh perspective on her situation.

"Ignore him," Ursa advised. "But at the same time, run into him every chance you get."

"But isn't that exactly what he wants? For me to leave him alone?"

"It is, but he can't recognize what he wants unless he's denied it."

"Kind of like what Ursa did with Reid," Tammy agreed. "She told him he couldn't have me, which in turn—"

"Made you more tempting. I get that, but Boris thrives on misery. He'll think by abstaining and suffering that he's doing good."

"So make yourself impossible for him to resist. You have a good figure," Ursa said as she eyed Jan. "Maybe a little skinny, but nothing a few pounds of cookie dough wouldn't cure."

Tammy snorted. "Trust me to find the one house where cookie dough cures everything."

"Lucky."

With a giggle, and a spoonful of batter, Tammy mmm'd her agreement.

Jan leaned her chin in a propped hand. "So dress sexy. Run into the moose. Ignore him. And hope that he what? Congratulates himself on being a blue balled, miserable jerk?"

"Much like a pressure cooker, the emotions and need will build in him until he explodes and carries you off for unmentionable things," Ursa elaborated with a wave of her wooden spoon.

"In other words, drive him crazy with lust until he drags you into a closet to have his wicked way."

Sounded fun, but Jan couldn't help but worry. "And if that doesn't work?"

Ursa and Tammy shared a look before saying at the same time, "Plan B."

"Which is?"

"Play dirty. Enflame his jealousy."

"From what I've seen," Tammy said, "it won't take much."

And if those plans failed, Jan could always resort to Plan C. Stripping naked again.

Chapter Fourteen

The doctor patched Boris up without any of the recriminations Jan had lavished on him. She didn't give him shit even though the wound had already begun to heal. She didn't harangue him even though it was tougher to remove the bullet because he'd waited so long. Doctor Weller knew better than to browbeat a man.

So why did he miss Jan's nagging presence?

Probably because he didn't have the hots for Doctor Weller—even if she was attractive with her curly red hair, bright smile, and curvy figure. In his world, only a certain blonde fox would do.

A fox who had disappeared and not kept him in the loop about her whereabouts. On the one hoof, he enjoyed the break. Keeping himself and his emotions in check when she was around took a lot out of a man. On the other hoof, though, who knew what the vixen was up to now? *Mischief, I'll wager.*

Exiting the clinic, he called his alpha for an update on what was happening.

Reid answered. "Boris, about time you checked in. You all patched up?"

"Good as new." If one ignored all his old scars.

"Excellent."

"Any new developments while I was seeing the doc?"

"Not really. We found the dead guy's sled hidden in the woods about a mile out of town. No trace of whoever took him out, though."

"Do you think it was Gene?"

"Could be. Whoever shot him certainly knew how to hide their tracks, but then again, any skilled tracker and hunter could do the same."

"Where do you want me to head now?"

"Home," Reid replied. "Get a few hours' sleep."

"I should head out now while the tracks are fresh."

"I'd prefer to have you fresh. I've got boys hunting for clues. If we find anything big, I'll let you know. Once you get a bit of shut eye, if the boys aren't successful, I'll want you and Brody to head out to the eastern ridge and see if you can't find out where the seal and the guy who took him out came from. The wind might have obliterated most of the tracks, but maybe if you loop out far enough, you'll catch some kind of clue."

"You think the seal was acting on someone else's orders?"

"I'd say that's a certainty. I mean, seriously, have you ever met a seal who had an original idea?"

Good point. Boris grunted in agreement.

"But, now the question is, who took the pudgy shit out? If the seal was following orders, then why kill him. Someone else was there. Someone who didn't want him to talk. It makes me wonder if we're dealing with two groups, or individuals."

"Two people making a play for power?"

Boris could practically see Reid's shrug. "Maybe. I can definitely say something fucked up is going on."

"I'll do my best to find out." And eliminate the problem.

"I know you will, but after you get some rest," Reid added, his firm tone brooking no argument. "You can drop Jan off at either Ursa's or my aunt's house to keep her safe."

A chill swept him that had nothing to do with the arctic temperature outside. "What do you mean drop Jan off? She's not with me." No, she'd stormed off without a word as to where.

"She's not? Oh. I just assumed. Never mind then. I'm sure she's gone to stay with someone."

Never mind? NEVER MIND! Someone stalked his little fox, and Reid didn't know where she was, and Boris was supposed to just forget about it? Forget about Jan?

Boris let out a bellow in the middle of the street that was more animal than man.

"Um, Boris, is everything all right?" Reid's voice emerged from the cell phone he still held in his hand.

"I'm fine," he bit off into the receiver.

"Didn't sound that way. As for Jan, you can stop worrying. Tammy just sent me a text to let me know Jan's at my place."

At least she's fucking safe. His relief was short-lived. "But you're not there."

"No, but Travis is around keeping watch. I never leave the house unguarded these days, not after what happened."

What happened was someone had dared once before to try and kidnap Tammy from Reid's place. They'd almost succeeded too. Thankfully, Reid arrived to the rescue.

Weeks had passed since without any further problems at Reid's home, but the clan alpha wasn't taking chances where his mate and grandmother were concerned. Someone guarded the place, and the women, at all times. People like Reid's cousin, Travis. But Travis was a young, hot-headed idiot. A good fighter yes, but one who didn't have the skills, experience, or training Boris and some of the other boys who'd served in the army did.

Maybe Boris should swing by and check on things. Make sure the young cub was doing an adequate job. A spot inspection. Yeah, just like his sergeant used to do.

Surely ensuring the safety of the Alpha's mate, grandmother, and foxy secretary were more important than him getting some sleep?

As for the mocking voice in his head that taunted him about his irrational need to check on Jan? He told his moose to trample it.

Before he headed over, he had one pit stop to make. Boris hitched a ride back to Jan's place where he'd left his truck and did a detour to his house on the outskirts of town. More like a cabin built in an A-frame style with a large picture window that spanned the main floor and extended up into the loft area of the second.

It was as he stuffed various weapons in holsters and pockets that he eyed the expansive view. What a perfect target he made for anyone watching. Good thing he'd invested in the toughest windows around. It cost him a ridiculous amount, but keeping his home open and airy, as well as safe, didn't have a price, not for a man who'd spent too many months in something only slightly bigger than a coffin.

Locking the door, and setting the alarm, which Reid had mocked him for when he'd first had it installed, Boris now thanked the foresight to make his home into a mini fortress. He had a feeling he might need it.

When he showed up at Reid's door a little while later, he didn't spot or smell any sign of Travis. Either the grizzly cub was well hidden, or shirking his duties. Boris hoped for the latter. Any excuse would serve to give the boy a cuff, under the guise of making him into a man.

Not that the boy would live to manhood once Boris got through with the womanizing little prick.

The sound of laughter brought Boris around from the front of the house to the back, where he found Tammy, Travis, and Jan bundled against the cold, but out in the open. Clear targets for anyone who came along. That was problem number one.

"Hold it steady with two hands, and remember, it's going to kick, so don't lock your arms too tight," Jan advised Tammy as she took aim at a tree—which looked remarkably healthy and unmarked despite the fact they'd chosen it for target practice.

Bang. The shot went high, and a branch quivered, sending a bucket full of snow to dump on the ground.

"Better," Jan said. "Now your turn, Travis."

"Watch this. I've been practicing." Travis took a wide-legged stance and held the rifle up against his shoulder. Barely taking the time to aim, he fired. And missed by a mile. "Dammit. I think the tree moved."

The women giggled.

"The tree didn't move. You're crooked," Jan told him. "Here, let me show you how you should hold the gun."

As Jan placed her body close to Travis', her hands over his, her breasts pressing into him, her voice low and encouraging, Boris felt himself detach from his body. It was the strangest thing. He knew on some level what he witnessed was perfectly harmless, but that rational-minded level wasn't the one in charge of him at the moment.

A more primal part of him surfaced, a possessive aspect to his personality that had, until now, remained dormant. It rose to the top, commandeered his limbs, and was to blame for the fist that met Travis' jaw when he spun around after his successful shot.

Did Boris feel bad when the cub's eyes rolled back in his head and he slumped to the ground? Nope. Damned fool had his hands on Boris' woman. He was lucky Boris let him live.

Unfortunately, Jan didn't quite see things the same way.

"What is wrong with you?" she exclaimed as she dropped to her knees in the snow beside Travis' prone body.

"Me? I was simply giving the boy a lesson."

"In what? How to survive a concussion from a rabid moose?"

"Bah, I barely touched him. Not my fault he's got a soft melon for a head. Besides, it would never have happened if he was paying attention to his environ. If you ask me, he got off lucky. What if I were the enemy? You all could have died."

"You moron. We knew you were there from the moment you pulled in with your noisy truck."

"So why didn't you acknowledge me?" Jan hadn't looked his way once. It was enough to prick a man's ego, if he cared about such things.

"Because I didn't feel like it," she retorted. "But if I'd have known being ignored would send you into a childish snit, I would have rolled out a red welcoming carpet."

Snit? Boris didn't have snits. He was a man, and a moose. He had episodes that some of his friends termed psychotic but he labeled stress relief. "Well, how was I supposed to know you knew I was there?" Given the convoluted direction of the conversation, Boris could feel himself going cross-eyed and possibly having another psychotic episode.

She didn't reply. Instead, she shot him a dirty look that said, "Really?" As if someone with her enhanced sense of hearing and smell wouldn't have known. Add in Travis' ability to hers and Boris' excuse was flimsy by any standards. But Boris blustered ahead. "Don't give me that look. Next time, if pretty boy here wants to avoid a nap in the snow, then he should do his job instead of screwing around."

"You better hope his mum doesn't hear about this."

The threat almost sent a shiver down Boris' spine. He'd heard the stories. He'd met the woman. With her plump cheeks, bright smile, and wicked wooden spoon, Travis' mom, Betty-Sue, appeared sweet on the outside, until you harmed her precious baby. Given her reputation, Boris, and many others, usually stayed far, far away. "Travis won't snitch." The cub knew better. The nickname momma's boy wasn't one he enjoyed.

"Hey, while you guys argue, mind if I go inside for some hot cocoa? My brand-new nose says Ursa has a pot of it ready, along with marshmallows." Tammy had only recently gone through the change from human to shifter. Given her human heritage and upbringing, she'd taken the news of her change rather well. She skipped off to the house, leaving Jan alone with Boris and a still snoring Travis.

Jan avoided looking at him, which irritated Boris for some reason. In the past, the few times they'd run into each other, she'd hungrily devoured him with her eyes, to his great annoyance. *I am more than a hunk of meat.*

Now they'd slept together, he expected her to… What exactly? Fawn over him? Simper? Throw herself into his arms and beg him to take her hard, fast, and furious?

She did none of those things. Not one. Nope, instead she practically ignored him, never meeting his gaze, maintaining her distance. Boris didn't like it one bit.

I am such a fucking idiot. One whom it seemed was never happy. He'd finally gotten his wish, for her to leave him alone, and now he wanted her focus back on him.

"What are you doing here?" he asked.

"I think that's a better question for you. I thought you were getting patched up," she said, scuffing the ground with her boots.

"I was."

"So shouldn't you be resting now?"

"Yes, but when I heard you were out here, and with your place currently off limits due to the fire, I thought I should drop by and give you this."

Somehow, this was not how he'd pictured this moment. Even as he'd stashed the box in his pocket, nervous about her reaction, he'd expected a more welcoming reception. Which he would have rebuffed, because, that was what he did.

At least his mention of a present got her to finally meet his eyes.

Wham! Dammit. What was it about her that always slammed him like a fist in the gut?

To hide the effect she had on him, he thrust out his offering.

"Is that for me?"

"Do you see anyone else around? Of course it's for you." He didn't mean it to come out so brusquely, but he couldn't help it. Jan didn't seem to notice. She took the gift from his hand and lifted the lid.

For a moment she was silent, but he saw how her eyes lit with appreciation, but it was her softly murmured, "Oh, Boris. It's beautiful," that just about sent him to his knees. "You got this for me?"

For some reason, he couldn't reply, only nod. He'd expected she'd like the gift even as he couldn't have explained why he got it. But the moment he saw it, all shiny and perfect, he'd known it would fit perfectly in her hand.

"Thank you." She cradled the nine-millimeter and rubbed its smooth, polished edge. "I can't believe the craftsmanship. The perfectly balanced lines. It's beautiful."

Just like you.

Ever since Boris heard the story of the gun her dad gave her, a gun lost in the ambush on her truck, he'd felt bad. He knew what it was like to have a weapon that was special. The perfect weapon you knew you could count on. The reminder of her loss came to mind when Boris happened upon the nine-millimeter as he browsed his weapons supplier catalogue.

Usually he would have just ignored it, the smaller pistol not exactly his style—he preferred something that could stop a marauding grizzly in its tracks. But something about it made him think of Jan; the sleekness, and perfection, the fact he could so easily picture her slender fingers gripping it.

Just like she gripped me.

Before he knew it, he'd ordered it for her, but then when it arrived, he sat on it waiting for the right moment.

"Ooh pretty shiny thing. Can I touch it?" a groggy Travis asked from the ground, his eyes slightly out of focus.

Their combined vehement "No!" settled that. That and the fact Jan cradled the gun to her breasts—breasts that pillowed his head less than a day ago. Sigh. He really needed to stop reliving that glorious moment if he wanted to have any hope of returning to life as he knew it. Boring, Jan-free, dull, and annoying life.

Travis rolled to his side before getting to his feet. He barely wobbled, and his eyes quickly regained their clarity. He rubbed his jaw and grinned. "Damn, Boris. You have got to teach me that left hook."

Did nothing ever crack the cub's cheerful mien?

Tammy stuck her head out the door. "Travis, your mother is on the phone. She said you needed to pick up milk on your way home."

"Yeah, I know. It's on my list."

"She also said you were almost out of condoms and should pick up some more. And to not forget her special cream for her rash."

Travis' happy grin dissolved in the face of Boris' mocking laughter. "It's not funny."

"Better run, little cub. Mommy needs you."

"What I need is to get my own place," grumbled Travis.

"So why don't you?" Jan inquired. "There are a few vacant units across the street from my place."

Travis sighed. "You really have to ask that. You have met my mother, right?"

Boris couldn't help but slap the cub companionably on the back. "Join the military, boy. It's the only way to escape a determined woman."

"And he would know," Jan said saucily as she tucked the weapon into her pocket. "Well, nice as this has been, I should take off now. Things to do, other people to see."

"Like who?" Boris asked. "And where?"

"None of your business."

When she would have stepped around him, he moved to block her way. "It is my business if I'm going to ensure you remain safe. Or have you again conveniently forgotten the stalker?"

"I haven't forgotten. Don't worry. If he turns out to be crazy, then I'll shoot him with my shiny new present. But if he's not, then I've got some sexy new lingerie that arrived in the mail a few days ago waiting for pickup at the postal office."

Wait, she'd ordered lingerie and planned on showing it to someone other than him? He could feel another rage coming on. Boris clenched his fists and pushed it down. Through gritted teeth, he said, "You still haven't answered me. Where are you going to stay? You heard the fire marshal. The roof for the entire townhouse needs replacing. You can't stay there."

She shrugged. "So I'll bunk with a girlfriend. Or here with the boss."

"No, you're not. You're coming home with me." Boris almost looked around to see who'd said it. Surely not him. Surely he'd not just invited the vixen into his home after all his grand speeches and reasons as to why he needed to stay away.

"No thank you."

He was about to recant his invitation when her words penetrated his thick moose skull. "What did you say?"

"I said no thank you. I am not staying with you. You've made it perfectly clear my presence is nothing but a hindrance. I wouldn't want to contaminate your man cave with my girly clinginess."

"I don't live in a cave." And he liked it when she clung to him.

"Doesn't matter. I'm still not going with you."

Never mind he'd not planned on bringing her home and was seconds away from uninviting her. As soon as she said she wouldn't, he decided she had to. What better place for him to keep an eye on her and make sure she stayed safe and out of trouble?

But she seemed determined to thwart him. She walked away, little ass swishing, blonde hair swinging. *She's leaving me.*

Once again, Boris the man took a backseat as Boris the cave moose trampled over. It took only a few strides to reach her and sling Jan over his shoulder.

"What do you think you're doing?" she squealed.

"Taking you home."

"I told you I wasn't going."

"And I'm saying you are."

"You are really tempting me to shoot you," she growled.

"Behave," he ordered.

"Or else what?" she sassed.

The temptation proved too much to resist. His palm smacked the tempting butt, which, if he turned his head, he could have taken a bite out of.

Jan screeched. "I can't believe you did that."

"And I will do it again if you don't start to listen. It's not safe right now for you to be wandering around. You will come with me whether you like it or not." He tossed her in the passenger seat, and when she crossed her arms and set her lips mutinously, he buckled her in— and yes, he took perverse pleasure in his arm brushing against her breasts. Then he went around and clambered in to the driver side.

"I don't appreciate you manhandling me just because I'm not doing as you commanded."

Funny, he truly enjoyed the manhandling part. Come to think of it, commanding her worked too. Of course, the kind of orders he'd prefer to give involved fewer clothes and her smiling around a mouthful.

"You weren't listening, so I took charge."

Jan made a rude noise. "I wasn't obeying because you're not the boss of me."

"No, but I am your protector."

"And who appointed you that? Reid?"

No one. Boris had appointed himself, but he didn't exactly mention that part. He remained silent and let her assume what she liked.

However this new Jan, this feisty Jan, this Jan who liked guns and shooting things, didn't want to leave things quiet. "Once we get to your place, I'm leaving."

"No you're not."

"And how will you keep me there? Going to chain me to your bed?" she asked sarcastically.

"If I have to." Again, with a preference of naked, which given her annoyance level with him right now seemed less and less likely. Probably for the best. *I'm not supposed to get involved, remember?*

"You know, for a guy who keeps repeating he doesn't want a girlfriend in his life, you keep acting like an awfully possessive boyfriend."

"Am not."

"Whatever. Stay in denial."

"I'm not in denial. I'm doing this purely for safety reasons. Since you won't take precautions, I'll take them for you."

"So you're not going to seduce my kidnapped body?"

"What are you yapping about now? I didn't kidnap you."

"Says the guy who threw me over his shoulder and ignored my protests. And I didn't hear you deny your plan to seduce me. Why, Boris, is this your sly way of getting me to your place and ravaging my body some more? You know, if you wanted me again so bad, you could have just asked."

Asked? Ha. Boris wouldn't ask; he'd take. But she was wrong. He wasn't doing this to seduce her—as tempting as it sounded. She'd soon see.

See fireworks apparently.

Chapter Fifteen

On the outside, Jan pretended indignation over Boris's treatment. But inside? Her fox was chasing its tail in giddy circles.

Boris could couch his actions in any excuse he liked. Jan saw through them. Her moose was jealous, possessive, and feeling a mighty urge to protect her. Oh, and let her not forget he would seduce her.

Whether he wanted to or not.

As soon as his truck stopped, Jan hopped out and began to quickly strip, in a feigned charade she would shift into her fox. As hoped, he caught her, slung her over his shoulder, and once again slapped her bottom—which acted more as foreplay than a deterrent.

She protested, a token protest of course. She'd always wanted to see where Boris lived, and where he slept.

He set her on her feet in his house, more of an open space with loft. She'd heard of minimalistic, but he truly defined it.

A simple kitchen lined the back wall, one long counter with pine cabinets below and above it. A white fridge and stove broke up the space as did the white, farmhouse sink with the window over it. A butcher block island with two stools acted as the only dining area. Not a man who entertained often.

A back corner was walled off with a single door, which she assumed led to a bathroom, or so she hoped. Outhouses weren't exactly high on her list of things she liked to use in the middle of winter.

When it came to furnishing, simple and sturdy seemed to rule. A thick, woven, brown plaid couch faced the large picture window. A scarred wooden table with scuff marks implied taking your boots off was optional. A standing lamp just behind an armrest, a surprisingly plush shag carpet of a deep blue, and a battered leather armchair finished off the living room.

"No television?" she asked, surprised at the lack.

"I hate falling asleep on the couch, so I moved it to the loft where my bed is."

The mention of his bed had her eyes traveling up the length of the open stairs, steeply inclined, to the platform area, which hung over the kitchen area. She could see the foot of the bed, the blankets neatly tucked under the mattress with military corners. Not for long, if she had anything to say, or do, about it.

She glanced from the bed to the massive window without shades of any kind. "Sunrise must be a bitch."

"I happen to like the light," he admitted. "Nothing better than waking up, the sun warm on my face, to remind a man he's alive."

"What about those of us who like to sleep in?"

"Since your staying here is only temporary and, given this time of the year, sunlight is only a problem if you're planning to get up late morning, I don't really see it being an issue."

Of course he wouldn't because he still persisted in his foolish belief he could live without her. Ha. Given his craziness back at Reid's house, apparently it hadn't occurred to him yet that he needed Jan.

Maybe I should try conking him in the head with a frying pan. It worked, after all, for Tammy.

Patience. She needed to slow down and exercise lots of patience. Boris was a stubborn moose. A man with mental wounds. The more she tried to force him, the more he pulled away. Her best results came when she denied him, when she let him think he'd lost her. Then the reluctant man turned demanding—and into an ardent lover.

"So how long are you planning to keep me prisoner here?" she asked as she wandered the open space. It saddened her to see how few personal effects littered the area. On the contrary, if she didn't know Boris owned this place since he settled here a few years back, she would have thought he rented it. No pictures on the walls. No knickknacks. Nothing personal to indicate a man of complexity and deep emotions—emotions he thought he hid—lived here. However, it did have one thing in abundance. Weapons.

Where most people would have hung a television, or some kind of art, he had a curved saber on two black metal hooks, the metal of the blade polished and gleaming, the leather-wrapped hilt, oiled and still supple. In the magazine rack tucked between his issue of *PC Gamer* and *Tactile Life* was a matte black Glock. *Nice.*

On a hunch, she flipped a couch cushion, and sure enough, there was a sheathed knife. It seemed they shared some habits. "Expecting company?" she asked.

"You never know," he replied, his hooded eyes tracking her every move.

"Personally, I like to have curtains in every room. Not only are they easier to keep clean than those mini blinds, which I swear are a magnet for dust, but my garrotes make great tie backs."

His lips twitched. "I keep mine on the key rack." He inclined his head toward it, and sure enough, hiding in plain sight was a leather knotted strip, with a key hanging off it. "But I like your idea. Maybe you could help me select some for the kitchen."

The import of his words struck them both silent. She, because she heard his inadvertent admission that he expected her to make herself at home, and to stick around. He because he'd obviously said something he'd never meant to speak aloud.

She did Boris a favor and didn't call him on it. Instead, she wandered to the door at the back and prayed for a true bathroom.

"Good grief, do you bathe your moose in there?" she exclaimed, opening the door.

"No, but I could, I guess. The shower is big enough."

Big, modern, and tempting, those words described the bathroom space. Unexpected did as well too. The entire space gleamed, from the striated marble tile on the floor to the big white tiles on the walls. To complement all the white, there was a thick line of river stone running down one wall of the shower and covering the shower floor. A glass enclosure surrounded it, no fog on the glass, which meant if she finished stripping and stepped in, which she did, there was nothing to block his view.

He gaped. He didn't drool, but only because he snapped his mouth shut.

But oh, how he stared as she turned the water on.

As she lifted her face into the spray, which started out cold and pebbled her skin, especially her nipples, he said, in a low, rough voice, "What the hell are you doing?"

"What's it look like I'm doing? Washing. As you keep reminding me, someone set fire to my house, and I stink of smoke. Then I lugged your sorry butt to the clinic. Then I played with guns. Not to mention, I got real sweaty last night doing some hanky-panky. I think, after all that, I'm in need of a nice," she turned to face him, "hot," she trailed a finger in a line between her breasts, "shower." She cupped both her breasts and aimed them into the spray.

He groaned. With her face in the water, lest he see her grin, she said, "Are you all right? Is something bothering you? Your wound perhaps?"

"Something is bothering me, but it isn't that bloody scratch," he growled. "I know you're doing this on purpose."

She let him see her smirk as she angled to peek at him through wet lashes. "Me? Would I do something like that? I thought we'd discussed the whole nudity thing before. And since that talk, you've not only seen me naked, but you licked just about every inch of my body." Again, she teased him, skimming her hands the length of her torso. His eyes tracked them, practically without blinking. "Given all that, you can't tell me the sight of my body is that shocking."

"You know what you do to me."

"No, Boris, I don't, because you keep telling me I'm not important to you and that you don't care." She threw that at him, and he reeled almost as if she'd physically shoved him.

"That's not true, and you know it."

"Do I? Tell me enough times, Boris, and true or not, I will start to believe it. You talk about being confused, well, welcome to my world. On the one hand, you say you don't want me, and yet, the way you look at me…"

"How do I look at you?"

"Right now? Like you'd eat me all up."

"Because I would," he admitted, so low she almost didn't hear him over the sound of the water.

"You look like you'd enjoy getting in here with me and pushing me up against this wall," she flattened her palms against the cool ceramic, "and pushing your big body against mine. Spreading my thighs," she placed her feet, shoulder width apart, "so you could thrust into me and claim me, take me, until I come, screaming your name." Closing her eyes, she placed her cheek against the smooth tile and thrust her buttocks out, rolling them slightly as if he truly did—

Oh my. She didn't even hear his clothes hit the floor, but he must have shed them because hard, hot flesh suddenly pressed against hers.

He growled against her lobe. "I might not be good for you. But god help me, I want you."

"Then take me." She uttered the invitation then immediately moaned as he nipped at her ear lobe, the flat edge of his teeth tugging the flesh while his hands spanned her waist. Calloused thumbs and fingers stroked at her skin while the hot length of his cock pressed against the crevice of her buttocks. Boris was a big man, and her body having tasted him once, practically melted into a paroxysm of delight knowing what to expect.

But he didn't immediately follow the course of her words. No, he had other ideas in mind. Decadent ones she approved of. He turned her so her back pressed against the tile wall. His lips left the shell of her ear and slid down the column of her neck, leaving a blaze of heat as he traveled. He ignored her aching breasts, his lips instead continuing their downward descent between their swells. Over her abdomen he kissed his way, lower still to the almost platinum thatch she kept short and trimmed over her mound.

And then, his tongue found her.

Say what you would, a man who knew his way around a woman's sex, how to tease it with the brief touch of a tongue, arouse it with warm breaths that raised anticipation, and a firm technique when it came to licking a plumped pussy, was a man to keep. *And I intend to keep him. You're mine, Boris. All mine, you and that decadent tongue of yours.*

Leaning against the wall, she thanked its firm support, else she would have melted into a puddle. Even then, she wasn't too steady, and she grasped at Boris' short hair, holding him as he ravaged her sex with his tongue.

She cried out, hips undulating in time to his wet strokes. When he inserted a pair of fingers, her channel spasmed, a wave of pleasure that had her squeezing tight.

On and on, she crested, the flesh of her pussy throbbing, pulsing as if it possessed a mini rampaging heart of its own. She felt swollen and needy, but more than that, as she stared down at Boris on his knees, his eyes closed in pleasure, she wanted to return the favor.

"My turn." She spoke softly, but he must have heard because he growled, "Not yet," against her mound.

She tugged at his hair, and he let go of her clit, which pulsed, and peered up at her with smoldering eyes.

She smiled and repeated, "My turn." She tugged his shoulders, urging him to stand, and he did, eyes locked with hers.

"What are you planning?" he asked.

Why tell when she could show him? She dropped to her knees and captured his bobbing cock. The flesh she gripped heated her palm, and it trembled. All of Boris trembled.

His eyes ablaze with tenderness and heat, he reached out and stroked her cheek. Just calloused fingers brushing her lightly, but that gentleness combined with his gaze? She'd never seen or felt anything sexier. It deserved a present. One he wouldn't forget, but certainly enjoy.

Leaning forward, she took him into her mouth.

"Oh, sweet fuck." Boris gasped as she deep throated him, her lips sliding smoothly back and forth, exploring the length of his shaft.

Suctioning pulled him tight, and each time, his hips bucked forward. He twined his hands in her hair, still gentle, not rough and demanding as she'd expected. It surprised her because she could feel him holding back. Holding back his need.

She didn't want him to exert control. For once, she wanted to see him let go. To fully embrace the moment. She started by letting him know how much she enjoyed the smooth feel of his velvety cock. Thick, long, and with silken steel for her to explore, she enjoyed the feel and taste of him. She made a sound similar to a purr but more rumbly, vibrating his shaft.

"Holy fuck, woman, you're going to kill me," Boris whispered.

"Not before you take me."

As if that were too much for him to ignore, he dragged her up and kissed her, his mouth hot and demanding against hers. "I'll take all right."

"Here. Now. In this shower."

"We'd never make it to a bed," he said with a grin that caused a mini spasm in her sex. How she loved it when he let go for just a moment. Cherished these glimpses of the man she first met a long time ago, when he still knew how to smile.

"Shall I bend over?" She peered at him through wet lashes and couldn't help but laugh at the astonishment on his face.

This time he was past words, although he might have grunted before he wrapped an arm around her waist. Hoisting her to waist height, she took it as an invitation to wrap her legs around his torso. It trapped his jutting cock beneath her butt where it rubbed, hot and hard, against her.

Lips locked, Boris leaned her up against the wall of the shower. His body pinned her, and a single arm remained locked around her waist. His hips undulated, seesawing his length against her. She trembled. How she wanted him to claim her.

And she was sure he would, eventually, once he was done torturing her. His free hand slid between their bodies to the folds of her damp sex. But that wasn't his goal. He found her clit and rubbed it, his thick finger pressing against her sweet spot. She keened into his mouth, his rumble of pleasure joining her cry.

While his thumb stroked at her clit, he slipped a finger between her plump lips. Then a second. *Oh my.*

When he added a third, stretching her, thrusting into her with his fingers, she trembled. Back and forth, in and out, the more he did it, the more she tightened, a most exquisite torture.

One that had to end.

"Boris," she gasped against his lips. "I need you. Please"

Actions instead of words. Boris guided the thick head of his cock and rubbed it against the entrance of her sex. She wiggled her hips, her silent way of saying "Hey, get in there now, please."

He chuckled. "Vixen." With that softly spoken word, and with a firm thrust, he sheathed himself.

Buried deep, his cock a pulsing hot and hard presence, he went still. But it didn't stop her from reacting to his beautiful size. She began to shudder, her sex contracting all around him. With both hands available, he shifted his grip so he held her buttocks while keeping her pressed against the shower wall.

With her firmly anchored, he began to pump, dipping his cock in, so deep, so fully. Then he slid it out until only the tip tickled the entrance to her sex. Then, he thrust, his dick slamming in.

"Oh god," she whispered.

He let out a moan, but he kept pumping, fast, hard, deep.

She dug her nails into his tense shoulders. A man on the verge, but determined to hold on and prolong the ecstatic moment. Again and again, he thrust. He pumped until she could hold back no longer for him, and she shattered.

The ripples of her climax milked his cock. Slamming it deep one last time, he held it there, letting her shudder in his arms and over his shaft. He bellowed as his whole body trembled.

They remained locked in a tight hug for a long while under the warm spray—which he told her later was courtesy of a well and a hot water on-demand system.

They embraced, lips soft and tender, bodies pressed tight, unwilling to separate quite yet. Jan savored the intimate moment.

I've claimed him. She might not have said any words, or left any visible marks on him, but she knew she'd imprinted his soul. Just like, knowingly or not, he'd put his mark on hers.

They might have a few bumps in the road to contend with, like Boris having a few more panic attacks about commitment. However, given how easily he seemed to succumb to his passion for her, she didn't doubt they could work through them.

Eventually, pruned skin and hunger prompted Jan to say, "Might be time to get out."

He sighed. "I know."

It seemed she wasn't alone in wanting the moment to last; however, this carnivore needed some protein.

They managed to eat before baptizing his kitchen counter. They made it to the bed finally but only because she had him chase her upstairs. Who knew fondling his big sword—the one on the wall—would arouse him?

The problem arose when it was time to finally rest and he went to leave her alone.

"Where are you going?" she asked as he sat on the side of the bed, groping for his pants.

"After what happened last night, I don't want to take a chance. I'll be on the couch or in my truck."

"Don't be an idiot. Stay here with me." Jan patted the pillow beside her.

"I can't. I could hurt you."

"Only if you can get to a weapon."

"Last time I used my hands."

"And I got free. But if it makes you feel better, which is your best hand?"

"My left."

"So we'll handcuff that one."

He blinked. "Excuse me."

Jan grinned. "You heard me. Where're the cuffs, Boris? I want to tie you up."

She did. And then she *did* him because, as it turned out, Boris harbored many a fantasy.

Sated, tired, and happy, she snuggled against him, ignoring the fact she'd had to handcuff him to the headboard.

But at least he stayed in bed. Stayed with her. And he slept. Nightmare free.

Chapter Sixteen

How did he manage to sneak into my home?

With the unmistakable sharp edge of a knife at his throat, Boris feigned sleep as he tried to decipher who'd managed to infiltrate his house. Someone stealthy because he'd not heard a thing. Someone with skills because his alarm system was pretty fucking hi-tech.

Whoever it was, they posed a threat, not just to him but to Jan, who wasn't presently in bed beside him. Sly little fox. He'd have to put a bell on her so she couldn't sneak around on him.

Breathing slowly and evenly, Boris maintained his pretense of slumber and tried to identify the scent of the person who'd broken in, but whoever debated slitting his throat wore a cloying cologne. A trick used by shifters in undercover situations to mask their scent. Just another clue indicating whoever he faced was not an amateur.

"I know you're not sleeping, boy," said a low-toned voice.

Boy? At thirty-something, people had long ago stopped referring to Boris as boy. Given the man wasn't fooled by his sleep act, Boris open his eyes and came face to face with a stranger.

Boris itemized what he saw. Almost white hair cut in a half-inch buzzcut, leathered skin that put the guy somewhere in his fifties, maybe sixties. A not-too-happy stranger in his mini fortress with a sharp knife against his throat and a coldness in his eyes that said he would slice.

And Boris, of course, still wore the bloody handcuff meant to keep Jan safe from his nightmares. Talk about ill timing. But he still had one hand free, if he could just—

"Daddy!" Jan squealed, popping into view. "What are you doing here?"

Boris froze. Daddy? Shit. This was bad. *So bad.*

The killer expression was replaced with a genial one as the male pulled back, the knife whisked away before an exuberant Jan threw herself at the short and slimly built male.

I must outweigh the guy two to one, and yet, he'd almost gotten the best of him. Oh say it like it was, the guy could have killed Boris before he said boo.

It made Boris want to jump from bed and pummel something. Or someone. Problem was, the person he wanted to pummel was hugging his vixen and asking if his Janny-girl was all right.

"I'm fine, Daddy. But what are you doing here? I thought you and mom were in Florida?"

"We were until someone called us to tell of the trouble you've been having."

"Nothing I couldn't handle."

"I hear you took a few of the scum out?" No mistaking the pride in his voice. She nodded, and her father grinned. "That's my girl. I want to hear all about it, but first, mind explaining what you're doing here with this beast?"

"He's not a beast, Daddy. This is Boris."

"The idiot who isn't good enough for you?"

"Don't start, Daddy. Boris has been nothing but great to me since this all started. He's been protecting me."

"Not too well if you ask me. I could have killed him while he snored."

"Oh please, Daddy, everyone knows you're the master of stealth."

Since her father seemed rather pleased with the compliment, Boris held back a snort. The guy boasted some serious skill, he'd grant him that, but to label him a stealth master? His old army buddy, Gene, might object to that.

"So how did you know where to find me?" Jan asked, sitting on the edge of the bed, not at all perturbed that she was having a conversation with her father while dressed in Boris' shirt. Rumpled hair, mussed-up sheets, not to mention the distinct eau de people getting it on, all screamed, "We had sex!" Boris was surprised Jan's dad hadn't slit his throat while he had a chance. *I doubt I'd be as restrained as him if it were my daughter.* A cute little girl with blonde hair like her—

Slam the door shut on that thought. He tuned back in to the conversation at hand.

"Finding you wasn't too hard," said her dad. "I called up Reid after I swung by your place and saw it cordoned off. Have they caught the little bastard who set fire to the place?"

"Jean! Language," warned a woman whose head popped into view. Lovely, another guest to join the party. Given her blonde perfection, there was no mistaking who she was. Jan's mother.

Boris thought himself well past the age of embarrassment until the woman's gaze found him still handcuffed to a bed, naked under the sheets. *Someone kill me now.*

A perfectly plucked brow arched as rouged lips tilted into a smirk. "Really, Jan, surely there are enough single men in town interested in you that you didn't have to resort to cuffs to get one to spend the night."

"Oh shoot. I forgot about that." Jan hopped off the bed and grabbed the key on the nightstand. With little decorum, she clambered back onto the mattress. She then crawled to straddle him in his shirt, which rode up her bare thighs as she leaned over to unhook his lock.

Given the circumstances, he managed to restrain himself from letting his free hand tickle up the length of naked leg. "What are your parents doing here?" he whispered.

"Are you deaf, boy? I said we heard about the fire," answered her father.

"We took the first flight we could find so we could come and support our poor, homeless baby girl."

Jan rolled her eyes, but from the tilt of her lips, Boris could tell it was more from affection than annoyance. To his surprise, Jan didn't move off him after she freed him but turned around to face her parents while sitting in his lap, which didn't improve matters, given his body had no sense where she was concerned. It went "Hello" under her sweet ass while he just wanted to bolt into the wilderness.

"Boris, I'd like you to meet my mother, Irma Benoit, and my dad, Jean Francois Benoit."

Irma waved, but Jean Francois glared, and when Jan turned her head for a second, Boris caught her dad making a slashing motion across his throat with one finger.

Definitely not making a good impression. And he'd better start sleeping with both eyes open. Or find a way to put a bell not just on Jan but also her dad.

When Jan turned back to face her parents, Jean Francois frowned at them. "You haven't answered me yet. Did they catch the arsonist?"

"Yes and no. We found a dead stranger who definitely smelled like he was there, that or he thinks smoke is a cologne."

"Dead? You killed him?"

She shook her head.

"So your boyfriend here killed him?"

Boyfriend? Now wait just a second. Startled, Boris might have said something if Jan hadn't quickly butted in.

"Nah, Boris didn't get a chance to take him out. But he could have," she said, rising to his defense. "Like I said, we found the guy, in the alley between the complexes. Shoved, it seems, from the rooftop and then shot execution style."

Her father couldn't hide his surprise. "By who?"

Boris uttered his theory aloud. "I think Gene did it."

Uh-oh. When that laser glare veered his way, Boris wondered if he should have kept his mouth shut.

"And who is this Gene person?" Jean Francois asked.

"An old friend of mine," Boris replied, unable to avoid answering.

"Who might be trying to kill him," Jan added.

"Nice friend," was her father's sarcastic reply.

"No worse than some of yours," said Jan's mother. "But we can discuss that over breakfast. I, for one, am starved. Your father drove like a madman to get here and then insisted we find you before feeding me. And I'm sure you'd both like to get dressed, especially your boyfriend, before his face gets any redder."

Before Boris could protest that he didn't blush, Jan's parents left, not far though, given the banging of dishes in his kitchen.

"I can't believe your parents are here," he whispered.

Jan didn't seem to give it the same level of calamity he did. "I know. Aren't they just great? I mean, who leaves an all-inclusive vacation in Florida to come back here just because of a few mishaps."

"Mishaps? Your life has been in jeopardy a few too many times now."

"Exciting, isn't it?"

He almost choked. "Jan, this isn't a game. Whoever it is we're dealing with, Gene, his buddies, or what not, they're serious, and deadly. You could have died in the crash or the fire. Just like you could have been shot."

"But I wasn't. Although you were. Not that your wound stopped you last night." She tossed him that special grin of hers, and his speech over how they shouldn't stay together evaporated. He'd broach it later. When he was wearing pants and she was wearing pants and her knife-wielding father wasn't in the vicinity. Somehow Boris didn't get the impression daddy dearest would handle Boris dumping his daughter too well—even if his intentions were good.

Whisking off the covers, Boris ignored Jan's whistle of appreciation, well, at least, he did. His cock, on the other hand, went to half-mast and bobbed in thanks. He would have thought with all the exercise it got in the last few days it would behave, but no, it really had a thing for Jan. *And so do I.*

Sigh. So much for keeping his hands off. There went that vow. As for keeping her out of his life? He no longer saw that happening. And now he had her family to deal with.

He began to understand how a condemned man felt as the noose tightened around him.

Dressed, armed—two knives, a gun, and a garrote for a tie, which dammit made it look like he was dressing to impress—he followed Jan downstairs to find her father on his couch admiring the rifle he'd had locked in his gun cabinet. It might have occurred to him to ask how he got his paws on it, but he didn't want to give the old man a chance to brag.

So Boris ignored Jean Francois, but he couldn't ignore Irma plating up pancakes and slices of ham—which she must have brought with her because he sure as hell didn't have that in his fridge.

Given his island was too small to seat the four of them, her parents sat on the couch while he sat on the armchair, and Jan sat cross-legged on the rug on the floor.

The food was great, even if he did almost choke on his fourth mouthful.

"We'll definitely need to get you a proper kitchen table and chairs if we're going to have some nice family dinners," Jan's mother remarked.

Jan pounded Boris on the back as he coughed, and rescue came from an unlikely source.

"Family? Who said anything about accepting this knucklehead into the family?" grumbled her father.

"Oh please. Anyone can tell he's smitten with her. Who wouldn't be? My baby girl is perfect."

It was Jan's turn to gasp and wheeze. Withholding a snicker, Boris patted her back.

"Of course, he's smitten. But it doesn't mean he's good enough for her. Or that I approve."

Irma snorted. "According to you, no one is good enough."

"I don't think it's too much to expect the best for my daughter."

"No, but given your standards are impossible, I'll settle for a man she likes. Some of us want grandbabies one day."

Both Jan and Boris just about died right then. Jan, once she stopped choking, managed to squeak, "Mom, we just started, um—"

She paused and gave him a panicked look, but Boris wasn't sure what to reply.

Exactly what had they started? Obviously claiming they were just fucking wouldn't go over well. Not to mention, even Boris had to admit they might have gone past that stage just a bit. Being a man of honor, he saved her and threw himself on the grenade. "We're dating."

With a smile of relief, and pleasure, Jan nodded her head. "Yes. We're dating. As in a couple. Boyfriend and girlfriend."

Her mother waved a hand and made a pshaw sound. "Oh, please. You can call it dating, but anyone can see you're meant for each other. Don't forget, I know who this boy is. I know what he means to you, baby girl. You know, if he's proving difficult to get to commit, you could always borrow the family shotgun. It is, after all, tradition."

"Oh Momma, really?" Jan's eyes shone, and she clapped her hands together in obvious pleasure. "I thought after you used it Daddy got rid of it."

"I tried," grumbled her father.

Irma casually stomped Jean Francois' foot. "As if I'd let him destroy a family heirloom. Never fear. I kept it safe just in case one day my baby girl needed it."

Confused, Boris leaned over and whispered to Jan, "What's the family shotgun used for?"

It was her father who replied. "It's actually a dual-pump action shotgun and, when wielded by a determined fox, means the end of life as you know it."

Jean Francois no sooner announced this than he reeled forward as Irma somehow managed to bop him in the back of the head while rising gracefully with her empty plate. "Do you really think that, my darling?" With a sweet smile husbands around the world knew to fear, Irma stared her husband down as she patted his knee. "You know, if you dislike your life so much, I could fetch it from the attic at Nana's house and use it one last time and give it a new name. The widowmaker."

"As if I'd die that easily and let you off the hook. You can forget it, wife. Just to torment you, I plan to live to be a hundred."

"Only if I don't poison you first."

As Jan's parents bickered, Boris found himself hyperventilating. *When did my decision to bed my vixen turn into me either getting mated or shot?*

And Jan, sweet, biddable, core-of-steel Jan, she didn't improve matters when she patted him on the cheek and muttered, "Don't worry too much about the gun. If you do force me to shoot, I'll aim for a body part that won't impede your ability to consummate our union or protect me."

With her laughter ringing in his ears, he fled for the wilds outside his home. But even under the vast sky, in the big, wide open, he could feel the walls closing in on him.

His vixen had set a trap, one that snared him and now threatened to spring shut, making him her prisoner forever.

But the scariest part is, I don't know if I want to escape.

Chapter Seventeen

Poor Boris. Jan let him flee, knowing she'd pushed him too far. But dammit, she'd never seen him so flustered, so panicked, so gosh darned cute.

Oops. I better not say that cuss word out loud, or Momma will have me spitting bubbles.

Jan carried their soiled plates to the kitchen. Her mother took them from her and shooed her away. Her father gestured she take a spot on a stool at the counter. Protest as he would that Jan's mother coerced him into marriage, her daddy was fiercely devoted to his wife and never strayed far from her side when he could.

"Okay, now that the beast is gone, tell me everything that's happened."

Sitting first, Jan did, from the attacks on Reid and Tammy to the destruction of her truck and home. She left nothing out, except for the seduction of a certain moose. Those details would only get Boris killed or, at the very least, maimed. Her daddy had a reputation, and he delighted in maintaining it. Thankfully, he and her mother had moved to a warmer climate years ago once Jan got her own place. But their frequent visits and phone calls kept their family bond tight.

As she finished relating the events affecting her and the clan, her father frowned. "By the sounds of it, there's more than just revenge afoot. Actually, if you ask me, it seems there are two separate agendas at play. One to undermine Reid as alpha of the clan and another to mentally torture the men who served with this Gene person."

Trust her father coming in from the outside to spot what they'd all missed. "We didn't think of that," she admitted. "We just assumed everything was about Gene's revenge."

"Sounds more like a cry for help if you ask me," interjected her mother.

"A cry for help that has seen people injured and killed?" Jan couldn't help the questioning note.

"I didn't say he wasn't violent about his methods, but I mean, look at it. What has the man really done that has actually hurt you?"

"My truck was destroyed."

"But you and Tammy weren't seriously injured," her mother pointed out.

"He sent shifters after me."

"Whom you killed and who probably had orders to simply capture."

"He changed Tammy from a human into a polar bear. Are you going to tell me that wasn't deadly? He could have killed her."

Her father answered before her mother could. "Actually, given what I've heard so far, this Gene person did Reid a favor. There's no denying that Reid marrying a human would have caused shi—" he cast a look at her mother, "um, trouble with the clan, especially the other clans who were hoping for an alliance. By changing Reid's mate into one of us, this Gene fellow made our alpha's decision more palatable."

"But she could have died."

"Highly doubtful. From what I hear, this Tammy girl is pretty strong mentally, to start with, which is important for the change. Second, we all know mates can't change their chosen one themselves. It's too much like inbreeding. I also know the stronger the blood of the shifter, the better the chances of the change working."

"I didn't know that," Jan replied.

"Of course not. It's not something bandied about because no alpha wants to deal with a randy boy who thinks the honey between the legs of a human girl means he should claim her. The decision to make new shifters should be treated with respect. Not to mention care. Can you imagine the chaos if we started turning humans left and right?"

A valid point. But Jan still wasn't convinced Gene wasn't evil. "Okay, so Gene suspected she'd live through it. From what I hear, the fight between him and Reid was fierce. Our alpha only survived by a miracle."

"I call bullshit."

Whack.

Her father glared at her mother, who smirked as she said, "Language."

"You're testing me, wife."

"And you're flunking, darling." Irma ruffled his hair, and despite her dad's growl, Jan could see he wasn't really mad.

"Gene's a killer," her father said, turning back to her. "If he'd wanted Reid dead, he would have shot him in the head. Instant death. But instead, he hits him in the shoulder."

"Like I said, he's crying for attention," her mother added. "However, that doesn't mean he's not dangerous. You'll need to guard yourself against him."

"I know Boris is convinced he'll keep coming after me. Boris thinks Gene is stalking me as a way of hurting him. It's why he keeps trying to push me away."

"And not doing a good job of it," grumbled her daddy.

"Jean Francois!"

"What?" her father said, trying and failing to sound innocent. "I'm just pointing out the obvious."

"Boris is still coming to grips with how he feels about me," Jan explained. "The war messed with his head. Just like it really messed with Gene's."

"I say we kill this polar bear threat. Lots of men suffered in the wars. Doesn't give them a license to act like," he cast her mother a look, "ill-bred louts."

Jan shook her head. "Whatever the case, this Gene fellow is making my courtship of Boris difficult. Boris thinks we shouldn't be together because I might get hurt by association."

"I think he should try harder to stay away," complained her dad.

"Oh, he's been fighting his attraction."

"But failing. That's my determined girl." Her mother beamed.

"I could almost feel bad for the guy when you both get that conniving smile."

"It's not conniving. It's fate," declared her mother.

"If you say so."

"I do. And that's final."

"Says who?" asked her daddy.

"Says me," her mother replied.

"You're bossy, wife."

"I know."

"So, what's the plan?" her daddy asked, idly playing with his knife, over, under, and around his knuckles, a hypnotic game she used to love watching when she snuggled on his lap, the mesmerizing play of light on steel lulling her to sleep.

"What plan? To get Boris to finally claim me?" Jan asked with a wrinkled nose.

"No. I'd say that moose is a goner no matter what he thinks or protests. I'm talking about a plan to trap this Gene person."

Her father thought Boris would succumb? Jan could have fist pumped in delight. She trusted her father's instincts. "Reid's working on finding Gene. He's got men out searching along with patrols."

"Bah, if this Gene is half as good as me, he'll have no problem getting past those. We need to set a trap and outfox the bear."

"But what should we use as bait?"

It didn't take their shared conspiratorial smile to come up with an answer.

Chapter Eighteen

An avid audience of one, Gene watched the comings and goings at Boris' house from the snow blind he'd erected. Seemed like a lot of visitors for a man who usually eschewed socializing.

Not so long ago, Gene thought he and Boris might have common ground. He'd noted how the moose kept to himself, heard the yells in the middle of the night, and spied as a wild-eyed man came running out the door to yell at the sky and shake a fist.

I'm not the only one with nightmares.

The thought strangely comforted him. Gene even pondered approaching Boris and opening a dialogue. But that was until he realized Boris was falling for the fox.

Suddenly, the man he thought he could unburden himself to, the person he'd most perceived as sharing his mental anguish, no longer seemed viable. Not to mention he'd probably try and kill Gene for toying with the blonde vixen.

It was what Gene would have done had someone fucked with a person he cared about. How he wished he could enjoy the comfort of a hug or simple caring human contact. As if that would happen now. He'd done so many things. Bad things. Evil things. Deadly things. Not all of them because of revenge, some in the name of survival, but still, there was no forgiveness for him. No warm homecoming.

He'd burned his bridges.

Alienated the people he'd once called friends.

Made an enemy of the one who dragged him from his self-made prison and promised him vengeance.

Gene had nothing left.

Nothing.

So why not end it all? End it now?

Because I'm not a quitter. Even if it killed him and the enjoyment was waning, he'd continue on with his plot for vengeance because at least when he fucked with his former comrades, he felt alive.

Even when dancing upon the tightrope of death, he had fun.

Too bad his balancing act required his old friends to fall.

Chapter Nineteen

With his home invaded, his mind in turmoil, and practically hyperventilating, Boris fled his house for the serenity of the woods.

Too much. It was just too much. Things were moving too fast. He'd gone from an imposed solitary existence to one with threats of not just marriage and permanence but family. Family dammit!

In his youth, Boris and his parents lived outside the shifter community, his mom and dad preferring solitude. But his isolation only lasted until the age of ten. A car accident took both his parents—damned semi truck wasn't paying attention to the sign declaring that stretch of the highway was a moose crossing. After their death, he went to live with his grandmother in her tiny apartment in Yellowknife.

The frail woman, who was already old when she got custody of Boris, was human. It was his grandfather who'd passed on his shifter heritage to Boris' mother. Being raised among humans, and by an older guardian, meant he never got to enjoy the warm, cozy, close-knit family gatherings most of his friends took for granted. Grandma tried, but with her health failing and living outside the clans, he never felt he belonged, anywhere. He swore she lived just old enough to see him graduate and enter the army before finally giving up on life, leaving him utterly alone in the world. Alone until he met his buddies in the army.

Always a bit of a loner, the guys he bunked with—Reid, Brody, Gene, Peter, Logan, and the rest of the boys—wouldn't let Boris remain aloof. They instantly adopted him as a brother, not just by rite of their sharing a shifter genome, but because, once a man had trained, sweated, and fought beside another, a bond was created. A bond Boris cherished because it meant he was no longer alone.

However, with caring came loss. Pain. The war took its toll on their numbers. Their capture by the insurgents and time spent in captivity stole even more.

In the end, Boris might have prevailed and escaped the camp with some of his army brothers, but the agony of those they lost was hard to shoulder. He almost let his grief consume him. He might have if Reid weren't determined.

"Come home with me," Reid said as they stood with their duffel bags over their shoulders, honorable discharge papers in their pockets, waiting for their flight back to the continent. They'd served their time, and done their duty to their country. The impetuous youths who'd enrolled had experienced life, both good and bad, and were now ready for something other than fighting.

"Kodiak Point is not my home." Nowhere was home. Just call him a drifter.

"You're my brother now, Boris. My home is your home. And besides, I could use you by my side."

Indeed, Reid could. With Reid's parents recently dead in a fluke accident, an opening for alpha of Kodiak Point was available. A natural-born leader, Reid was more than suited to the task, and Boris would gladly work for him.

Yet Boris hesitated. He hesitated because he feared. Feared remaining with these last few men he cared about, and feared even more the girl he'd once met in Kodiak Point. A girl he'd made a promise to when he was still just a boy. A promise he had to break because damaged men didn't get a happily ever after with the girl of their dreams.

In the end, Reid got his way. Damned alpha trait. Reid wanted Boris' help, and he couldn't say no. So he traveled to the remote town in Alaska and took the position as clan enforcer. Grew to love the place and its people, but he stayed far, far away from the emotional entanglement he saw in a certain vixen's eyes.

It hurt. Oh how it hurt so much more than expected and it had taken strength to keep himself from succumbing to her allure, but Boris managed for years. The nightmares helped as did the daily reminder of the pain of losing someone close. He thought he had things under control, and while not exactly happy, he could say he'd achieved a certain level of contentment.

And then she went and ruined it all by smashing through his self-erected barriers and worming her way into his life—and heart. Now Boris wasn't sure he could ever let her go. In denying himself, he'd done the one thing he'd sworn not to do. He'd hurt himself. But most of all, he'd hurt her. Not physically, but emotionally. *The one thing I was trying to prevent.*

Not to mention, he'd lost a battle. He'd let fear win.

However, there's nothing to say I can't have a rematch. Slowly, Jan was learning about his issues. They didn't daunt her. Bit by bit, he was learning she was tougher than she seemed and able to handle him. The excuses he'd made for remaining aloof were getting dismantled, and he no longer could deny his need for her.

But what if I lose her?

Then again, it wasn't just death that could take her from him. If he didn't act, another man could claim her. Jan wasn't the type of woman, as she'd already indicated, to spend the rest of her life alone. If he didn't find his balls—which were massive as a moose but tucked away when it came to committing—then he'd find himself losing her anyhow.

Could he handle Jan with another male?

Fuck no. I'll kill any man who touches her.

Guess that answered that question. In that case then, he'd better moose up. Or, as his old sergeant used to say, "Suck it up, you panty-wearing, pansy-assed woodland creatures, or I'll shoot you myself and stuff your heads for my wall." Given the bastard was a crazy fucking rhino, no one doubted for one moment he would do it. Damn how he missed his sarge.

The cool temperatures and his internal pep talk calmed him down enough to realize he would accomplish nothing walking around in circles in the snow. He retraced his steps and noted the white Dodge Ram pickup still parked in his driveway, which meant Jan's parents hadn't left.

Great. Boris couldn't have said what bugged him more, the fact Jean Francois had caught him unaware and thought himself better than Boris or the fact the man didn't think he was good enough for Jan.

I'll just have to prove him wrong on both counts.

Apparently, Boris spent more time in the woods than he'd initially thought, long enough that when he returned to his house it was to find her parents making themselves at home. Jean Francois had dismantled a few of his guns and cleaned them while Irma was buried inside his stove, scrubbing.

Invasion of the foxes. A horribly scripted B movie unfortunately featuring him.

The one shining light? Jan.

Sure, he still believed he wasn't good enough for her. And yes, he still feared hurting her, but given all that happened, a few things became clear as he took his walk through the woods. Ready or not, Boris could no longer fight fate; Jan and her blasted family were here to stay.

Not just because the vixen was stubborn but because Boris could finally admit—just not out loud yet—that maybe, just maybe, he needed her in his life. Maybe.

Peering around, he frowned when he realized he couldn't spot or scent her. "Where's Jan?"

Jean Francois didn't bother looking away from his polishing of the barrel on the magnum. "Out."

"Out? What do you mean out? Where?"

"Said she had to meet with an old friend to help put a ghost to rest."

Oh tell me she didn't. Boris slammed a fist down on the butcher block hard enough to make everything on it rattle and bounce. "And you let her go?"

"Jan's a big girl. Besides, she went armed."

"To track down a psycho."

"What are you talking about, boy?" Jean Francois met his gaze.

"I mean the ghostly old friend is Gene. She's gone to find him. Stupid, stubborn vixen."

"Be careful what you call my daughter. And I'm sure you're wrong. She wouldn't have gone to find a killer without inviting her father. She knows how I enjoy a good hunt."

Boris also knew she thought she was invincible. "So does she."

"What are you going to do about it, boy?" Jean Francois fixed him with a stare.

"Find her and bring her back, of course."

"Would you like some rope?" her mother asked. "I've got some in the back of the truck."

"Rope?" Boris was visibly startled at the suggestion. "What for? I wasn't planning on tying her up."

Jean Francois snickered. "Not for her, you bloody idiot. For the fellow she went looking for. Unless you want him dead. If that's the case, then Janny will take care of him."

"Think she'll bring back the pelt?" her mother mused. "I've always wanted a polar rug."

"You do know this is a man we're talking about, right?" Boris snapped.

"A man you claimed has gone psycho. A man you say threatened my Janny. Does this mean you're not going to kill him when you locate him?"

"If on the off chance she has found him, and he hurts a hair on her head, I can promise you he won't live to see another day."

"Then if that's the case, I see no problem with requesting you at least try to kill him in polar form. What?" exclaimed Jan's mother when both men stared at her. "Just being practical. Their fur is awfully soft on the toes."

"Damned crazy woman. Always sleep with one eye open," Jean Francois advised. "Always."

With that advice ringing in his ears, Boris slipped back outside, but not before tucking a second gun into the back of his pants. He also grabbed his keys. He slipped outside, only to stop, stymied by the fact all the vehicles remained in the driveway. Which meant…

Sure enough, he noted a neat pile of clothes on the porch, which he'd missed on his way in. Jan had shifted. There wasn't much light coming from his home, but he had enough to see the tiny paw prints in the snow.

"You've got to be fucking kidding me." The vixen, who had obviously inherited her father's insanity, had taken off on four feet.

For a moment, Boris debated going inside and recruiting her dad. The man might not sit so complacently if he knew his daughter had ditched her gun along with her human layer to go after a predator a zillion times her size.

However, Boris was a man—with the card to prove it! Men, especially the shifter type, had too much pride, especially when it came to asking for help—*and no way am I asking her dad who already thinks himself better than me*. Besides, Boris wanted to be the one to rescue Jan if she was in danger. There was no guarantee of that if dear daddy came along.

With only a slight grimace at the cold, Boris shed his gear before morphing into his moose. As always, the pain of transformation was quickly forgotten with the exhilaration of his other shape.

He knew some shifters thought him unlucky in his animal. They considered a moose less noble or cool than other animals. He disagreed. For one, his massive shape wasn't something trifling. A full-grown bull moose could tip the weight scale with many a large predator. The fact that he didn't sport pointed teeth or claws didn't mean he wasn't a force to be reckoned with. There was power in his limbs. A grace in his stride. And he'd always secretly thought his rack, which spanned close to six feet now, was fucking awesome. Say what you would, but when he struck a pose, Boris knew he appeared majestic.

And not just because his nana used to say so.

With a ripple of the thick winter fur lining his body, he took off with a steady gait, following the tiny fox prints, which twined and wound through the woods. Then abruptly disappeared.

What the hell?

Boris swung his large head from side to side, wondering if he'd missed a rocky outcropping she could have leapt to in order to throw him off his path. Nothing. Just pure unmarked snow, if one ignored the marks he'd made lumbering through.

It made no sense. Jan couldn't fly. He sensed and smelled no trace of another. Just crisp, fresh air.

So where did she go?

He belted out a challenge, hoping for a reply. Nothing echoed back.

Somehow, his vixen had managed to slip away and not leave a track.

Impossible.

A dusting of snow, dislodged from a branch overhead, made him blink. And then he blinked again. An idea formed, but he almost discounted it. Surely she hadn't.

He craned to peek and sure enough, the fluffy white draping some of the boughs was disturbed.

I'll be damned. Daddy taught her well indeed.

Most shifters, when they transformed, preferred to do so with all their feet, er, paws or hooves, firmly planted. But that was a personal choice for balance and to make it easier.

However, it wasn't necessary, and if one had the skill of being able to act whilst going through the transition, it sometimes meant the difference between life and death in some situations; hence it was a skill many in Boris' platoon practiced. Not him. With four hooves and a balance dependent on them, Boris never shifted anywhere but firm ground.

But for someone agile, and wily, springing into the air whilst changing to grab hold of a branch and swing themselves up so as to not leave footprints in the snow? If anyone could swap from animal to human while mid leap, Jan could he'd wager.

Damn.

Finding Jan had just taken on a whole different level of difficulty. Tracking her route through the treetops was practically impossible. She could have gone in any direction. His only hope was naked human skin in the cold was sure to drive her to ground in short order so she could warm herself with her fur. Problem was choosing which direction to go.

Would she have doubled back after leading him away so she could hop into a vehicle and take off? Would she rely on her four legs, and occasional two, to get where she thought she needed to go?

This time when he bellowed, the frustration clearly marked his tone.

When I get my hands on her, I'm going to tan her ass until she can't sit for a week. No, make that a month. Of all the stubborn, foolhardy things she's done so far... This one frightened him the most.

Boris didn't know where Jan was. No one did. She could be in danger. Hurt. Captured. Drinking hot cocoa, snickering. Waiting for him naked in bed. Or yelping in the distance?

The unmistakable cry sent a frisson throughout his body, and unmindful of what he ran toward, he took off at a trot. Forget prudence and watching his steps. Jan was hurt and needed him.

His antlers tangled in some of the lower branches, snapping the icy boughs like matchsticks. His breath steamed in the cool air as he ran, and his ears strained to hear another sound, another cry, anything to guide him.

When the figure leaped down to the ground from a large conifer in his path, he almost ran right through him. Someone stood in his way. Move it!

He skidded to a halt at the last moment and took in the details of the intruder in his woods. Well, his woods so long as he kept making payment each month to the bank on his mortgage for the hundred acres he'd bought.

The stranger was dressed in white camouflage, including tinted goggles, and carrying a rifle, military grade Boris judged, given it was a prototype he'd read about but wasn't available for the general public. It didn't take his well-equipped nature for Boris to know whoever he faced wasn't an ordinary hunter.

Nope. Nor was he a stranger.

When a white gloved hand raised the goggles, Boris couldn't have said he was surprised to see Gene. But the man facing him, the man scarred by experience, was not the Gene he'd known. And by scar he didn't mean the one bisecting Gene's face.

There was a hardness to his features, a cruel tilt to his lips and a coldness in his stare that didn't exist before. Before Boris stood a man who'd suffered, and from his experiences, emerged tougher and more deadly than ever. Add to that slightly insane.

This could have been me, had Reid not dragged me back from the brink.

Unmindful of the cold, Boris swapped shapes and growled, "What have you done with her?"

"Is that all you have to say to the friend you left behind?" Gene replied with an arch of a brow.

"Don't start with that crap. You and I both know if I'd had an inkling you lived, I would have stayed and looked for you."

"Start with that crap? Challenging words from a guy suffering turtle dick to someone holding a gun."

So uncool. It wasn't Boris' fault his cock and balls were tucked in as far as they could go to avoid the bite of the arctic temperatures. "Where is Jan?"

"Ah yes, the lovely little vixen. I can see why you're taken with her. Such lovely flawless skin. Her hair, a sheen of silk. And that body." Gene licked his lips. "A part of me wishes I'd stayed instead of leaving that note the other day. Perhaps then it would be I sharing her bed instead of a backstabbing moose."

"You leave Jan alone."

"Such jealousy. Does the little fox mean that much to you then?"

Admitting she meant everything to him might paint a larger target on Jan, but denying it could mean lessening her importance in the grand scheme and costing her life if Gene didn't think she was a viable hostage.

"She's my mate." He admitted the one fact he'd tried to deny for so long out loud to the last person he would have expected to.

Gene appeared surprised. "A mate. Oh my. Even with all your flaws? Absolutely amazing."

"Enough yapping. It's fucking cold out here. I don't know what you want, but leave Jan out of this. Swap me for her. Let her go. She shouldn't have to pay for my supposed transgressions against you."

"How noble of you, old friend. However, you're accusing the wrong person. I'm not the one who has her."

"Not you? Then who?"

"Would you believe me if I said pure evil? Or at least its henchmen."

"You're not making any sense. Do you mean one of your guys has her?"

"I have no troops. No one to aid me. Not anymore at any rate. The person I initially began working with had a difference of opinion with me. Needless to say, we're no longer talking."

So there was another person also orchestrating attacks. Good to know, and he'd have to inform Reid, once he found his vixen. "You think this guy took Jan?"

"I don't think; I know. I saw a pair of his hunters tag your fox with a tranquilizer and cart her body off."

"And you did nothing to stop them?"

Gene snorted. "It is you who would act the part of hero, not me. I merely observed."

"You fucking prick. No, make that a coward." Boris didn't care if he stood naked and that parts of his body were going numb. He also didn't give a fuck Gene had a gun and who knew what other weapons stashed on his body. This asshole let someone take Jan. *My vixen.* "The old Gene I knew would have never let anyone hurt a hair on a woman's head."

"The old Gene died overseas," he hissed.

"Bullshit. You escaped."

"But not unscathed, or did my new facial marking escape your attention?" Gene indicated the silvery scar that bisected his brow, wound down across his cheek, and slashed the edge of his mouth.

"We all have scars. And as Travis would say if he saw yours, and not without envy, chicks dig scars."

Gene snarled. "But they don't enjoy nightmares or a man who wakes screaming or sobbing every night."

"Some do. Jan doesn't mind." Which still amazed him.

"But I mind!" Gene roared and swung around, his bare fist connecting with the bark of a nearby tree. The coppery taint of blood from torn knuckles filled the air, as did the despair of a man certain all was lost.

Boris understood that, but he couldn't deal with Gene's issues now. Not with Jan in the hands of the enemy. "Listen, I understand you're hurt. That's fine. You want to lash out at me, and Reid and the other boys, that's fine too. However, can it wait until I've gone to rescue Jan? She's innocent in all this. She deserves better."

"Better than you at any rate," Gene mumbled.

Boris nodded. "On that, you and her dad and even I are agreed. But she's a stubborn little thing, and sweet too. Whatever this evil dude wants with her, she doesn't deserve it. So let me go, just for now. Let me rescue her fluffy white butt from whatever trouble it's in now, and when that's done, you and I can tangle."

"You assume yourself capable of rescuing her."

"I have to be." Anything less than success was unacceptable.

"And if you're not? You would deprive me of my vengeance."

"Glad to see your priorities aren't skewed," was Boris' sarcastic reply.

"Don't talk to me about priorities. I've fully admitted I'm a dick but a dick who's still going to help you against the guys who took your girl."

"Why, so you can stab me in the back when I least expect it?"

"I might have lost a lot of things overseas, but I have a small shred of honor left. It's grain sized, but when I say I'll do my best to help you save this chit, you can believe it. I want your undivided focus when you and I battle, face to face."

"Old-school knuckle fight like we used to do in the barracks."

"Except, this time, we won't stop at first blood."

Healing quickly didn't mean they pounded on each like psychos, but they did like to push their limits. Abuse their bodies in a controlled environment so they were better equipped to deal with pain later. "Deal. Let me hit the house and grab my gear, and we'll go after her."

"There is no time for that. We must catch them before they leave these woods. Once they enter *his* sphere, we won't stand a chance, and your mate will suffer because you had to stop to get some pants."

It went against his better judgment to listen to Gene, but if the bear spoke honestly and something happened to Jan because Boris had wasted time? "Shut up and lead the way," he growled before switching back into his moose.

With Gene setting the pace, Boris put his trust in the buddy they all used to call Ghost. No matter where they were, Gene had an uncanny ability to blend into his surroundings. One would think a man close to seven feet with shocking white hair and a bulky body to make most NFL recruiters salivate would stick out; however, Gene was a master at camouflage.

When they'd landed overseas, dropped from a wilderness they understood into an arid place full of rock, sand, and hard-packed dirt, they'd all felt like walking targets. Except for Gene. Before twenty-four hours had gone by, he'd adapted his gear to blend into the environs, never mind it meant he got reamed by their commanding officer because his idea of blend meant he'd dipped his fatigues in the gray dust of the place and had dyed his boots a shade of brown.

Lest you think his skills only pertained to outdoor camouflage, it should be noted he did just as well in populated areas. Less than a week after their arrival, there was a point when no one knew where the ghost was, and speculation abounded he'd gone AWOL.

Boris wagered against that and won a tidy sum. He knew Gene would never just up and leave. He was right. It seemed Gene had slipped into town wearing native garb and facial makeup. The intel he gathered more than made up for the laps around camp and the pushups their CO ordered when no one could report his location.

Ah, the good old days, before shit happened.

As Boris watched his old friend jogging, his compact snowshoes barely stirring the snow, he wondered how long he'd been watching, spying, waiting for his chance. The most disturbing part? Boris never even suspected.

How many opportunities had Gene let lapse to take him out from afar because he wanted a face-to-face confrontation?

Or did he?

Boris really had to wonder what Gene's true purpose was. Did he truly want to see them dead, or was this just the desperate cry of a man looking for someone to blame and hurt? Someone to share in his pain.

Gene was who Boris could have become if not for Reid and the others. *And because we left him behind, he feels betrayed.* No wonder he wanted vengeance. Here they'd gone on with their lives while Gene languished, a prisoner still. It made Boris feel guilty to realize they'd assumed the ghost was dead. *He's right. We are assholes because we never even looked.*

We owe him.

So Boris would trust Gene to help him save Jan, then he would give his old friend the fight and closure he needed afterward. Hopefully it wouldn't be to the death. Maybe he could convince Gene that he didn't need to live as an outcast and strike from the shadows.

But only once Jan was safe.

Boris didn't need Gene's flashed hand signal to know they neared their quarry. The idiots weren't making any attempt to hide their presence, not since they'd joined with a larger party of thugs.

And thugs were what they were. It didn't take a genius to recognize the unwashed, scruffy men grouped around a half dozen snowmobiles were the rejects of shifter, and human, society. Bound by one common purpose, violence and chaos, they joked amongst each other about the fine bonus they would receive for snaring the white fox the boss wanted.

While their voices carried in the still woods, they'd yet to realize they had company. Hell, they didn't even have someone on watch. Cocky and sloppy.

If this were a training drill, the sarge would have been tearing them a new asshole. How he missed the man—like he missed a deerfly nagging at his haunches. Not!

But back to the ill-trained louts. Between the shadows hiding Boris' presence and Gene's ability to blend, it was easy for them to creep closer to the makeshift camp the intruders had established, one which they currently dismantled.

As Boris took careful steps, closer and closer, he marked off the enemies' position. Six snowmobiles, facing outward in a circle, kind of like the wagons of the old Wild West circling and providing a false haven.

In the center, a fire glowed, gel fed by the smell, which meant no smoke carried on a breeze to give them away. Hitched to the back of one of the snowmobiles was a trailer upon which was strapped a cage, a fucking cage of all things, and captive within it, the still form of his vixen, the bright tuft of the tranquilizer dart still sticking out of her snowy white side.

Her confinement and their cowardly methods angered him, but the fact he could see the subtle rise and fall of her chest, signaling her living state, kept him from going berserk. But not by much.

These assholes would pay for touching her. Pay with their lives.

The lack of breeze made it hard to discern what type of shifters he and Gene faced. In total there were ten men. By the disparaging remarks— *"Stupid skin walker"*—Boris assumed at least two were human. One was definitely lupine, and in need of a bath, but as for the others, who knew? Who cared? Their lives were now measured in minutes.

Of more concern than their animals' shapes, was their armament. All sported some kind of weapon—rifle, shotgun, several handguns. One even carried around a crossbow, which Boris personally found kind of cool. Anyone could shoot a gun, but it took skill to take an animal down with just an arrow.

Given the firepower and numbers against them, Boris now wondered if he should have taken the time to outfit himself with some artillery instead of his rack. Yet if he had, as Gene surmised, they would have missed them. As it was, the enemy group was already almost done packing up, and the engines were revving, warming up in preparation for departure.

Swapping skins so he could communicate with words instead of snuffles and grunts, Boris used the noise of the motors to cover his whisper to Gene. "I don't suppose you've got any moose armor in that backpack of yours."

Before anyone laughed, the military had equipped Boris in some during their training, black Kevlar type prototypes. While he proved more effective in human shape wearing battle armor with a gun in each hand, some of his other friends found the animal armor useful.

Brody, a wolf, enjoyed the lightweight suit as it deflected knives and bullets while he tore his way through enemy ranks. And there was something freaky about a Kodiak bear, standing on its hind legs, wearing a superhero-type suit.

"If I'd have known *he* bolstered their numbers since the last sweep, I would have let you put some pants on. But it's too late now. I've got an extra gun, but no clothes, unless you want a blanket."

"What the fuck would I do with a sheet? Fight toga style?" For some reason this pulled Boris' lips into a wry grin. "No thanks. I'll take my chances as a moose. Got anything in there though that we can use to blind them or at least distract them enough for me to get close enough to do some damage?"

"That I can do." Gene actually grinned as he pulled a handful of stun grenades from one of his many pockets. Loud noise, smoke, and a bright flash. Perfect when a man needed a bit of chaos. "But before I toss those into the ring, what do you say we even the odds a little."

Unslinging his rifle, Gene took a position on one knee and aimed. Shivering and not needing to watch, Boris already knew Gene would hit what he targeted. The man was an excellent marksman, something Boris was counting on. He also counted on the fact these ill trained louts would suck when it came to target practice, or at least not hitting anything vital.

As the first shot Gene fired hit its target, head shot so no getting back up for that one, Boris swapped back into his moose in time to hear the shouts.

"Holy shit, someone's taking potshots at us."

"Jacob's down."

"Use the sleds as shields."

"Open f—"

The command got lost as Gene tossed the first mini bomb into their midst. Boris had just enough time to shut his eyes against the bright flash, but he couldn't stop his ears from ringing at the sharp pop that probably echoed for miles around.

Good thing he didn't need to hear to fight. While the kidnappers milled about in confusion, he charged in, taking advantage of their disorganized state. Not military trained that was for sure. His old sarge had taught Boris and the others too well to fall for such an obvious baiting tactic.

Rack lowered, he plowed into the first body he spotted. Lift and toss. It didn't kill the fucker, but it got him out of his way.

With smoke from the grenade stinging his eyes, Boris waded into the fray while Gene picked off from the outskirts.

Did Boris worry Gene would mistakenly nick him? A little, but of more concern was the wild shooting of the idiots within the circle of snowmobiles. Jan still lay listless in the cage, vulnerable to a stray missile. It put him in a difficult position. By placing himself as a shield in front of her did he make her more of target for those bullets?

Probably, so despite all his protective instincts that screamed he should get close to her, he remained on the opposite side, drawing their fire and, for the most part, remaining unscathed. Well, not completely. He bore some furrows and scratches from near misses, but no actual dead-on hits. You could arm idiots with guns all you liked, but unless they spent time practicing, they were better off using their natural-born gifts.

It seemed the idiots came to that conclusion too, as many ditched their weapons and swapped human skin for fur and, in one case, feathers.

Seeing the giant eagle poised to take flight, Boris mentally cursed. He didn't want the bastard to fly off and possibly warn, or worse, bring back more buddies to help out.

But how to stop him?

Gene appeared suddenly at his side, a ghost manifesting. Pulling out a knife, he drew it back and let it fly. The dagger flew with unerring accuracy and took the giant bird in the throat before it could take off. Gagging and flapping its wings, the eagle danced around in the throes of death.

"I don't know about you," Gene said, turning to face him for a moment, "but I'm thinking about fried chicken for dinner tonight."

If Boris could have laughed, he would have. That macabre remark in the midst of battle was so something the old Gene would have said. Surely, once this was all done, there was something they could do, something to—

A bullet nicked one of the tines on his antlers, ruining its perfection.

Fucker.

Boris bellowed and went after the prick. A trample of his hooves made the shooter regret his lucky shot.

The screams and yells diminished, as did the smoke. As the circle they battled in calmed to a certain degree, Boris realized they'd just about vanquished the group.

Sensing their sure defeat, a chubby-cheeked seal shifter, whose gun clicked uselessly, flung the empty weapon at him and turned to run for the woods. Boris ignored him as he saw Gene effortlessly jogging after him. The ghost wouldn't let him get away.

Which left him with his sleeping vixen, Jan. Oh and one crossbow-wielding asshole who stood in front of the cage aiming at him.

The term hitting the side of a barn came to mind as the little shit grinned and aimed right for Boris' chest.

Damn. *This is going to hurt.*

Chapter Twenty

When Jan went for her walk in the woods, she'd meant to draw Boris out. To scare him a little, and yes, perhaps have him experience an AHA moment where he realized how much he loved her. Or wanted her. Something.

She'd not actually expected to run into trouble. Like a foolish kit, she'd trusted the fact her daddy approved of her plan to frighten Boris to mean there was no actual danger around. Boy, would she ever give him heck when she got out of this mess. And she'd also mock him for not having realized there were enemies in the woods.

But that was later. This was now, and now consisted of her waking from a tranquilizer, stuck in a cage, a dog cage of all things, while some kind of battle raged around her.

The good news was whomever managed to get the drop on her was getting their ass handed to them. The bad news was Boris was bleeding from several wounds, superficial ones, but still, these jerks were hurting her moose!

And me without a gun to shoot them.

Lying low in her cage, lest she get inadvertently struck by a stray shot, she took furtive peeks to see if there was anything she could do to help the situation.

Luck was on her side. Once again, they'd underestimated the tiny little vixen. The guys who captured her relied on the simple locking mechanism for the cage, no padlock in sight.

There was just one problem. She'd need human hands to manipulate the latch, which given the size of the cage, would not be fun.

However, when the jerk with the crossbow took a stance in front of her and aimed, she knew she had to act. Shifting while tucked into a ball was not the most pleasant thing she'd ever done, nor was the biting cold any gentler than when she'd done her arctic dash through the treetops, but the "oomph" of pain when she brought her knee up between the unsuspecting crossbow guy's legs? Totally worth the hard nipples that could have poked holes through glass.

Of even more worth was how quickly her moose swapped fur for skin to sweep her into his arms, his naked, if cold, body welcome against hers.

"You came for me," she murmured against his chest where he'd smooshed her face.

"Of course I did, even if you should have never gone off by yourself in the first place. You little idiot, what were you thinking?"

"I was trying to prove a point."

"What point was so important it was worth risking your life?"

"Making you understand I meant something to you."

He sighed. "And you couldn't find a less dangerous way?"

"I'll admit, kidnapping might have been a tad extreme, but the better question is did it work?"

"You know I care about you."

"Enough to stop pushing me away?"

"Maybe."

She shoved at his chest. "What do you mean maybe?"

"I still don't think I'm good enough for you."

"Your opinion in this doesn't matter," she retorted.

"Your dad agrees."

"My dad has no say in my life."

"And neither does your moose." The intruding speaker interrupted their private conversation. The stranger, clad in white snow gear from head to toe came closer and it didn't take a sniff for her to realize she was finally meeting the infamous Gene she'd heard so much about. "I upheld my side of the bargain, Boris. Time for you to keep yours."

"What's he talking about?" she asked, worry threading her tone along with icy fear as the man began to strip off his holsters and various layers.

"In exchange for his help in rescuing you, I agreed to a fight," Boris explained.

"A fight?" She stared from the man she knew could shift into a polar bear to her Boris, who while strong and dashing in his moose form, was no match. "Are you fucking insane?" She ignored the imaginary taste of bubbles in favor of a word that fit the situation.

"I owe him this," Boris said softly, reaching out to brush his thumb across her cheek, wiping a tear she didn't even realize had fallen.

"But he'll kill you."

"Thanks for your confidence," was his wry reply.

Realizing she couldn't reason with Boris, she turned to Gene. "Why? Why are you doing this? Why can't you leave him alone? Don't you know how tortured he is already by everything that happened to you guys over there?"

"Tortured?" Gene sneered. "Ooh, he has nightmares as he sleeps in his cozy bed, in his nice house, with his perfect life and mate. Did he and the others care that they left me in the hands of those bastards for years? He doesn't know the meaning of torture until he's spent years, not months, in the hands of the enemy."

The pain in Gene's eyes tore at her, but the insanity frightened her. "But it wasn't his fault," she cried, already knowing her plea would fall on deaf ears.

"I don't care. I've got nothing left to lose. I only live for vengeance."

When Jan would have argued further, Boris drew her shivering frame into his arms. "Run now, while I distract him."

"Not without you."

"Let her watch. Then she can tell the others what to expect when I come for them." Gene's lips twisted. "I can promise you my version of justice will be kinder than what *he* has planned."

"Who is this he you keep referring to?" Boris asked as he picked among the dead bodies, pulling off jackets and sweaters. He tossed the smaller items to Jan, who grimaced but pulled them on to her chilled frame. Dead man gear might not appeal, but losing limbs to frostbite would suck even more. To her surprise, Boris also pulled some of the garments on. Was he planning on retaining his man shape then for the duel? He might stand a better chance if he did.

"The one I speak of is pure evil," Gene said which coming from him didn't bode well.

"You've said that before."

"He's also the one who saved me in the end, even if he was no better than my captors."

"But who is he?"

Gene raised haunted eyes to meet Boris' gaze. "He is a part of our past. The bane of our present and death in our future. I made a deal with the devil, and the devil reneged. But I won't let him steal my soul, not until I've had my revenge."

And with those cryptic words, Gene, dressed lightly and unarmed, charged Boris.

Chapter Twenty-one

As Boris met Gene's polar rush with a grunt of exertion, he wished he could have convinced Jan to go. While Boris might stand a chance against his old comrade in a bare knuckle fight, he'd end up fucked if Gene swapped into his polar shape. Unless Boris cheated and went for a gun.

Some would say Gene didn't deserve any courtesy, that if it took Boris fighting dirty to win, then he should take the chance, no matter the cost to his honor. If it were any other asshole, Boris might.

But this was Gene. Gene who'd slept in the bunk under his and used to poke him with his rifle butt when he snored. Gene, who made the human recruits piss themselves by shifting into his bear form, looming over their tents and roaring. A man Boris had once shared a hole in the ground with as enemy fire peppered the dry and dusty land. A friend he'd shared beers with and swapped rations—your shoe-leather fruitcake for my cherry-and-fruit mushy medley. Gene was more than just a fellow soldier and a friend; he was practically family. *Once upon a time, we were like brothers.*

So as much as Boris wanted to live, he would play fair. He would give Gene the fight he wanted. He exchanged meaty fists with his lost pal, their bare knuckles bruising with the force of their blows.

Boris caught some of the roundhouse kicks aimed his way and pivoted to throw a few of his own. He swept his leg as Gene paused to wipe streaming blood from his eye, the cut on his forehead gushing—damned scalp wounds; they made things so messy. His move took Gene off guard, but not enough that he didn't grab at Boris so they both tumbled in the snow.

For a few minutes, they rolled around on the ground, staining the packed snow with their exertions. They grappled themselves upright and continued their violent dance. Together, they panted, sweated, exerted, evenly matched and neither gaining the upper hand.

Which begged the question, why wasn't Gene killing him? Boris knew he could. He'd seen his old friend take out the enemy with one well-aimed chop to the throat, and yet, Gene kept holding back, not going in for that killing strike.

But he sure was leaving his mark on Boris. Bruises blossomed all over his body. A rib or two, maybe three, cracked during a particularly vigorous hug that had Jan shrieking.

"Stop," she cried. "You're killing him." Followed by the more worrisome click of a hammer being pulled back. "Let him go," she demanded, "or I'll blow your head off."

Crouched in a fighting stance, Gene didn't take his wild, angry eyes from Boris' as he snarled. "Stay out of this fox. This is between Boris and me."

"I won't let you kill him." She took aim, and Boris knew she'd do it. Solve the problem for him. Take the decision from his hands.

"No," Boris yelled. Despite the fact he left his rear unprotected, he lunged and knocked her hand as she fired, skewing the shot.

With a yelp, she turned hurt-filled eyes his way and whispered, "Why?"

Gene replied for him. "Honor. It always was his failing. But not mine."

The kick to his back sent Boris flying face first into the snow, but even blinded, he heard Jan's scream.

"Leave him alone," she yelled.

As he pushed himself to his knees, he saw Jan attack Gene, her little fists pummeling him, ineffectually, but in her terror-stricken rage, she didn't seem to care. She jabbed her knee upward, and missed. She tried to headbutt; however, Gene tilted his head. With someone less experienced, his vixen might have done some serious damage. Not Gene though.

"Enough," roared the polar, a hint of animal growl coming through. He flung her away from him, and she stumbled and tripped over a body. She fell hard, her head cracking against the side of a snowmobile.

That berserker rage Boris had thought all used up in the initial battle? It returned. And forget his previous notions of honor. No one, old friend or not, touched his vixen. "You. Hurt. Jan." The words were roared as Boris sprang to his feet and lunged, hitting Gene in his midsection and tumbling them both to the ground. Straddling the bear's upper torso, Boris pummeled him.

Left. Right. Left. His primal inner beast enjoyed the satisfying smack of flesh on flesh. It took several shots for him to realize Gene did nothing to defend himself. He didn't fight back, which totally took the fun out of it.

Chest heaving, Boris paused in his beating to stare.

Gene lay on the dirtied snow, bruised, battered, and bloodied. He didn't beg for mercy. He didn't raise a hand to protect himself. On the contrary, he kept his arms spread in a gesture of surrender.

As Boris panted in the cool air, his warm breath misting, he could see Gene wanted to die. Saw the defeat in his eyes. The silent demand to put him out of his misery.

Killing Gene would solve so many things. Giving him the bullet he desired would end a large portion of the problems facing him and the clan. Best of all, it would make Jan safe, from Gene at least. But ... Boris couldn't do it.

He knew what it was like to live with the nightmares. To wake screaming at ghosts and to alienate himself from those who would dare care about him.

In a sense he was Gene, or would have been were it not for Reid and the others. They'd brought him back from the brink of despair and given him purpose. And then Jan brought color and warmth back into his life.

Knowing how close to the edge he'd once tread, could he really condemn Gene? Or was there another way?

He stood and gazed down at Gene. He could see the resignation in his old friend's eyes. It would be so simple to give him what he wanted. Life was full of hard choices. Try or die. Kill or let live.

Boris held out his hand.

But Gene wouldn't take it. He slapped it away. "What are you doing? Shoot me. You know it's the only way. I deserve this. I brought this on myself."

"I won't kill you."

"You have to. Think of all the things I've done. The people I've hurt."

"We all make mistakes."

"I'm made more than mistakes." Gene yelled. "I deserve to die for what I've done. I should never have come back. I should have died in that damned hellhole."

It hurt Boris to hear Gene's truthful admission, the pain in it. "Yeah, you've made mistakes. Bad ones. But so did I. We all have at one point or another. Sorry, old friend, but you won't be dying today. It's time to put the past away and move forward. Time to heal."

"Heal? Are you out of your fucking mind? I. Tried. To. Kill. You." Gene enunciated each word. "Avenge yourself."

"I forgive you." Three simple words. Words that made Gene physically flinch as if each were a bullet.

"No. No. NO!" Rolling to his knees, Gene pounded at the snow and screamed wordlessly. Boris didn't let that stop him from putting his hand on the man's shoulder. A simple touch. A touch not of violence but of forgiveness and acceptance.

"Nooooo!" Gene roared, the tone shifting into a mighty bellow as his polar bear burst free from his human skin in a frenzy of white fur. Off Gene lumbered, his head shaking wildly as if trying to dislodge a coronet of bees, but it would take more than that to shake the unleashed emotions loose.

Watching, Boris made no move to follow. Had he made a mistake? Perhaps, but more and more, as he looked back upon Gene's actions, while destructive and hurtful in nature, a part of the bear had held back from the final step. Yes, he'd done vile things, but in the end, he'd not crossed the last threshold where redemption was no longer possible.

In the shifter world, wild instinct often battled with civilization. Violence, while not as a widespread, was still a huge part of their lives, so it made them perhaps a little more understanding and willing to forgive or avenge slights. Did Gene deserve punishment? Yes, but somehow Boris doubted anyone could punish Gene more than he punished himself.

Boris turned as he felt Jan's light touch on his arm. He tucked her into his side, relieved that, in spite of a blooming bruise on her temple, she didn't seem any worse for wear.

In a soft voice she said, "Are you sure you should let him go? He did, after all, harm people in the clan."

"He lashed out. But honestly, if you look more closely, those who were most hurt were those acting against us. What did we lose? A few traitors, a roof, the blinders we wore thinking our clan was insulated from the bickering so often found in other shifter groups. If Gene deserves to die, then so do I. I've done bad things too."

"For the good of the clan," she said justifying his actions.

"A matter of perspective." The families of those Boris harmed and killed for the good of the clan would argue he was evil and in need of putting down. How events were perceived depended on which side of the battle lines one stood and how the outcome affected you.

"Will he be back?"

"Yes." Of that, Boris was fairly certain. "And maybe next time I will have to give him the death he begged for, or maybe, now he knows he can still achieve forgiveness he can begin the process to heal."

"Or go completely postal."

Perhaps, but Boris wanted to believe that at his core, the good Gene, the one he used to trust with his life, was still somewhere within the broken shell of the man. He hoped.

With nothing left to keep him out in the cold, Boris commandeered a snowmobile and bundled Jan on the back, but not before snagging a cell phone from a body and putting a call in to Reid.

He relayed the events to his alpha quickly and without embellishment. At the end of it all, Reid sighed. "Are you sure letting him go was the right thing to do?"

"Maybe not for the clan, but it was for me," was his honest reply.

"Then we'll deal with it. I'll send a bunch of guys out to your location for cleanup. Will you be sticking around?"

"I'd rather not. I want to get Jan away from here before she causes more trouble."

"Hey," she chirped with a slug to his arm. "If it weren't for me, you'd be wearing a crossbow in your heart."

"If it weren't for you, I'd be home, warm and snug."

She made a face at him as Reid cleared his throat. "If you two are done bickering..."

"Sorry. You were saying."

"I was asking if you have a clue as to who Gene meant when he talked about this other dude running his own agenda?"

"Nope, other than the fact it's someone we might know. Someone from our past."

"But who?" Reid asked.

Who indeed? A question Boris would worry about later. Right now, he had a shivering vixen to get home.

Dragging their asses back to his house on a snowmobile that chugged like a tired choo-choo, Boris fought to remain alert. Not easy given he was tired and bruised. But not beaten.

They'd emerged victorious this day. *We're alive. Intact. And going home.*

He didn't even have the strength to muster any surprise when he saw the white pickup truck still sitting in his driveway.

It seemed he still had guests. Great. He opened the door to his house and ushered Jan into the warm interior.

Jean Francois was just helping Irma into her coat.

"I told you the boy would bring her back," he remarked to his wife.

"How do you know it's not she who dragged him back?" she retorted.

"Why is it you don't seem surprised by the fact we both look like we've engaged in a minor war?" Boris pointed out.

His accusation froze Jan who stood in front of the fire warming herself. She turned to face her parents, her gaze narrowed with suspicion. "Daddy, when you sent me outside to run around in circles and worry my moose, did you know there were rogues in the woods with a tranquilizer gun?"

"Yes. I knew you'd find them." Jean Francois didn't even have the courtesy to appear abashed at his actions.

"They shot me and kidnapped me. If Boris hadn't arrived in time, I might have ended up who knows where. Maybe even dead."

"But you didn't. I figured the boy would find you."

As their conversation filtered through his tired brain, a kernel of anger sparked. "You mean you intentionally sent her into danger?" Boris bellowed.

"She wanted you to get it through your thick skull you cared for her and needed her. I thought it would do her some good to also see she needed you. If you ask me, it all worked out in the end."

His "She could have died!" was echoed by Jan's "He could have died!"

United, they both faced off against Jean Francois, who shrugged. "Such drama. I would never have let things go that far. Or did you not wonder why ten armed men never once managed to hit your ridiculously big and clumsy carcass, boy?"

It was then Boris noticed the snow melting from Jan's dad's boots. "You were there?"

Irma snorted. "Of course he was. You didn't seriously think he'd trust another man with our daughter's safety, did you? As soon as he sent you after her, he picked up Jan's trail and shadowed her the entire time and made sure nothing bad happened to her until rescue arrived."

"If that's the case, then why didn't you show yourself during the battle?"

"I wanted to see how you'd acquit yourself. I just stayed on the outskirts and took care of anyone who might actually get lucky. You didn't do too bad for a moose," was the grudging admission.

"Oh, Daddy. I should have known you wouldn't let me down."

Boris could only gape as his vixen hugged the grizzly fellow, who smirked at him over his daughter's shoulder. But he couldn't be mad at the man, not if his unseen aid kept everyone alive.

"I knew your moose would come to the rescue. Such a dashing figure you must have presented with your large rack," Irma said as she flung her arms around him. For such a tiny woman, she packed quite the vigorous hug.

Unsure of what to do, Boris awkwardly patted her back, but blushed beet red when she cupped his jaw and kissed him soundly on both cheeks. "Welcome to the family, son."

Son? Boris practically choked. Jean Francois went into a coughing fit. "Son? Son! I never said I gave him permission to have my daughter," the older fox argued as his wife tugged him out of the door. "Don't I get a say in this?"

"No," Irma replied just before Jan closed the door, leaving them alone for the first time in what seemed like forever.

"Are they always like that?" he asked.

"Yes. Aren't they great?" Jan beamed at him.

Great wasn't the word he'd have used. Faced with such a bright smile, Boris held in his sigh. Alone and unsure of what to do next, he proposed the most obvious. "We should shower."

"You better not be implying I stink."

Boris couldn't help the tilt of his lips. "You might not, but I certainly do. And it seems such a shame to waste all that space and water."

"So you're doing this for efficiency?"

"No. I just want to get you naked." He couldn't help a grin at her dropped jaw.

"Why, Boris Sobolev, did you just proposition me?"

"Yes."

"But what if I'm not in the mood?" The devilish twinkle in her eye said otherwise.

"Then I guess I'll have to convince you."

"Now that sounds promising," was her husky reply as she leaned back against his fireplace mantel with her arms crossed.

He leaped over his couch and managed to make her eyes widen in surprise, but it was her soft gasp as he literally tore the salvaged clothing from her body that sent lust surging through his loins.

"I still can't believe," he said as he braced an arm on either side of her bared body, "that you actually jumped around like a squirrel from branch to branch naked." A sight he really wished he could have seen.

"Not for long," she admitted. "It was freaking cold. But I didn't want to make it too easy for you."

"Am I going to have to chase you often?"

"What do you think?" was her giggled reply as she ducked under his arm and bolted, nude and gorgeous, across the room to his bathroom.

Tearing at his own borrowed clothing, Boris shed his layers as he followed. He entered the washroom to find her already standing in the glass enclosure, the water running. With a seductive smile, she crooked a beckoning finger.

As if he needed an invitation. He entered the shower and immediately enveloped her in his arms. But she held back, her fingers tracing the myriad bruises and cuts covering his body.

"You're hurt."

"I am. And some wounds might never heal. But when you're around, I don't feel them. For some reason you make me feel whole again."

"Because you're mine," she claimed possessively as she drew his head down for a kiss. It began as a soft embrace, a sensual slide of lips against lips. But Boris wanted more than that. Despite his fatigue, a wild instinct to claim pulsed within him.

He needed to make this woman his. His in a way everyone would identify. His so she would never question his commitment again. His so he could finally stop dreaming, and enjoy the reality.

Her lips were pliant to his demanding kiss and needed little coaxing to part. A grunt of satisfaction left him when her arms came around him, clasping him tight, firmly pressing her body flush against his.

With more force, his mouth pressed hard against hers, and he slid his tongue into the warm recess of her mouth. But he wasn't the only one who could claim. Her mouth pressed back just as firmly, her tongue dueled just as wetly, neither conceding the upper hand, both determined to leave a mark. A sensual mark.

Her shorter stature meant she had to crane and stand on tiptoe to fully taste him. How adorable she was. He lifted her off the floor with ease, pushing her back against the shower wall, bringing her to just the right height for him to grind his pelvis against hers. The way she moaned and arched, her nails digging into his shoulders, set his blood on fire.

Control slipped from his grasp, and Boris didn't bother to chase after it. He wanted the passion to overcome him. He needed it. *I want to feel alive.*

As her limber legs wrapped around his waist, locking him against her, he felt her molten core press against his rigid cock, which was trapped between their bodies.

How can this feel so fucking good? He'd not even sunk inside her yet, but he knew how it would feel and looked forward to it. The heat of her clinging to him, squeezing him, welcoming him, and only him.

Mine.

Impatience and need made it impossible for him to wait any longer. *I need her. Now.*

Into her snug, wet sheath he slid, and despite his strength, the pure pleasure of it almost sent him to his knees. He took a few shuddering breaths as her channel gripped him tight. He adjusted his hold on her, cupping her sweet ass cheeks, giving himself leverage.

"Boris, I need you." She made the soft admission just before she nibbled at his neck.

Holy fuck. Was it her words or her gentle bite that enflamed him? Who cared? He flung his head back. The cords in his neck bulged with the strain of holding himself in check. All of his instincts screamed at him to pound her sweet and willing flesh, but he was more than just an animal driven by primal urges. He was a man, a man determined to make his vixen cream.

With her back pressed firmly against the tile wall and his hands still cupping her perfect ass, he pumped into her willing heat, hard and fast. In slammed his cock, then out, the seesaw motion a sensual delight for them both. How moist she was. How hot.

His dick had never felt so full, so ready. He gasped as her sex gripped him tighter than a vise. He almost lost it. He had to stop his thrusting to regain some control over the situation. It made her mewl and squirm. She sat on the edge of bliss, needing just a little push to send her over. He tilted his angle of entry and slowly pushed in and out, really grinding the tip within her. When her channel convulsed, he knew he'd found her sweet spot.

Nails clawed at his back as he bumped the head of his dick against her G-spot, over and over.

"That's it," he crooned. "Come for me. Scream for me." Let her orgasm and spread her lovely cream all over his cock.

A moment later she came. Her sex convulsed, moist flesh pulsing around him, fisting him and drawing forth his own climax. He couldn't help but bellow her name as he came, his seed, his mark, bathing her womb even as he nipped at her neck, the flat edge of his teeth pinching the skin.

She cried out again, a second orgasm rippling through her, and he just about hit the floor as his knees threatened to buckle with the bliss of her pleasure.

With the hot water streaming over their heaving bodies, he cradled her close, determined to never let her go. To never let her come to harm. To never let pride, an enemy, or even her family come between them.

For better or worse, you are mine.

Chapter Twenty-two

Rolling over in the obscenely large bed, Jan made it to the other side before realizing she'd awoken alone.

Well, that sucked. Given the tumultuous events of the day before, and then the wicked lovemaking, there had been little time for talk with Boris. Or should she say have a discussion about their future?

While Boris had said some pretty sweet things, she still worried about his level of commitment.

Would he decide to run? Try to shut her out? Pretend once again she didn't mean anything to him in order to spare her from his personal demons?

I hope not. But knowing her honorable, and idiotic, moose, the possibility definitely existed that he'd try to pull the martyr act. Would she ever get it through his thick skull, no matter what demons haunted him, she wasn't going anywhere?

She groaned as she buried her head in the pillow, but only until she heard his mocking, "Hey, sleepy head, are you planning on lying in bed all day? We need to hash some things out."

Speaking of her moose...

Rolling onto her back, she smiled at the sight of him, relaxed and shirtless at the foot of the bed. Smiled, that was, until he leveled a familiar shotgun in her direction. "Boris, what are you doing? And why do you have my mother's gun?"

"This?" He wagged the barrel. "Irma called this morning while you were sleeping, and we had a bit of a chat. Nice lady your mom, by the way."

"Yes, she is, but that doesn't explain how you got your hands on the family shotgun."

"She was kind enough to drop it off for me."

Narrowing her eyes, she asked, not without suspicion. "Why?"

"I'll tell you why, if you give me half a chance." He cleared his throat, and was that nervousness she perceived in his eyes? "Jan, you drive me bloody mental and not always in a good way."

"Oh really? Did my mother also happen to bring a shovel because, so far, you are digging a pretty big hole?"

"I wasn't done."

"Then get to the point," she teased, curious, and hopeful as to where this conversation was going.

"I'm trying to get to the point. So stop interrupting, or I'll get the duct tape."

"Kinky."

"We'll get to that later. Anyhow, as I was saying, you drive me crazy, but you also make me feel great while you're doing it, which I don't quite understand."

"I still don't get what me driving you bonkers has to do with you aiming a gun at me."

"Because you won't stay quiet long enough for me to get the words out. And you know how I hate talking."

"Not around me you don't. If you ask me, you talk too much and don't act enough," she grumbled, anxious for him to get to the point— and better yet, get those jeans off him and drag him back to bed.

He cocked the shotgun and yelled, "Quiet, woman. Can't you bloody well see I'm trying to propose to you?"

Her mouth snapped shut, and she blinked at him.

"Jan Marie Benoit, I tried to fight it. I tried to ignore it. I tried every fucking thing I could to get you out of my mind, but dammit it all, I can't. You're a part of me, a necessary part, and while I think you could have done better, and your dad insists you should, any attempts by any other man to do so would have probably ended up in murder because I can't stand the thought of you with someone else. I love you, Jan, and you will be my mate and wife. Even if I have to shoot you and drag you to the altar to get it done."

Elation bubbled in her. He loved her. *He loves me!* And yet he pointed a gun at her? How utterly Boris. "You wouldn't shoot me."

"Okay, maybe I wouldn't, but I sure as hell won't take no for an answer."

"Hold on, if you never planned to shoot me, then what's the gun for?"

"Well, according to your mom, it's tradition in your family to use it. So I thought what the hell. I mean, I like guns. You like guns. I like aiming guns. I like you." He shrugged and grinned. "What better way for me to get engaged than at gunpoint?"

"You do know the tradition in my family is for the women to wield it or their daddies."

"I hate tradition for one, and secondly, I never wanted you to doubt I wanted this. I never want you to think you had to force me because, when it comes to you, I would suffer anything, your parents, your irritating need to interrupt, your ability to find danger, even a chain around my ankle and a bloody white wedding in a church if you'll only promise to stay at my side."

A smile tilted her lips, and her eyes surely sparkled with mischief when she said, "My mother will make you wear a tux."

He winced. "I survived the army and various forms of torture. I'm sure I can survive that."

"We'll have to have the ceremony outside because my hillbilly cousins like to get drunk and shoot things when they're celebrating."

"So long as they don't shoot you, we're good."

"I want a honeymoon on a beach."

"Argh, woman. With sunshine and sand? Don't you know how that blasted stuff can chafe a man's sensitive parts? Can't we just go camping in the woods and find ourselves a cozy cave?"

She arched a brow.

He made a face. "Fine. You win."

Actually, he would win big time. Just wait until he saw her itty bitty bikini. She could almost wager she'd never make it to the beach.

But she wasn't done torturing him. "One last thing, when we have a daughter—"

"Daughter?" His eyes widened. "You mean as in us, having children?"

"Yes, children. I'm going to want a couple."

"A couple?" He gulped.

Oh, how cute. The big bad soldier was afraid of kids. "At least three. Maybe more. But we can decide on the actual number later. Anyhow, I am warning you right now, Mr. Cave Moose, my girls will be taught to shoot guns just like the boys."

"Why on earth would they need to know how to shoot a gun? I'll be their daddy. If anyone goes near them, I'll protect them." He puffed out his chest. Mmm. Such an impressive chest.

Not quite done though, she explained. "While they might have big, bad Boris as their daddy, that won't give them the skills they need to fend off teenage boys."

His eyes widened. "Teenage boys? Near my girls?" Despite the fact these supposed daughters didn't exist yet, she could already see the idea settling within him and rousing the family man—and protective father—instinct. Totally sexy. "Teenage boys are randy little pervs. On second thought, we'll need to teach my girls more than just gunplay. I think we should plan on some hand-to-hand combat, definitely some knife work. How young can we start them? Never mind. I'll ask your dad. He'll know."

As Boris planned for the future, Jan couldn't help but grin. Not so long ago she'd despaired of the man she loved ever realizing they were meant to be. But, lucky for her, one big, stubborn moose had gotten outfoxed by love.

And now that she had him in her life, nothing, not even his past, would ever keep them apart.

Or they'd face the wrath of a rabid snow fox, and her extended family. Which, given the long winters, was quite big. And vicious. On second thought, bring it. They could use some excitement for the next family reunion.

Epilogue

How long he ran, Gene couldn't have said. But no matter how far and how long he fled, Boris' damning words rang through his head.

"I forgive you."

The nerve of the moose. As if he had anything to forgive. If anything, Boris should have begged Gene for forgiveness. Instead he'd apologized and absolved him.

Who the fuck did that? Gene had done bad things. He'd intentionally set out to hurt the men he once loved as brothers. He'd generated terror and pain and fear among the people living in Kodiak Point, all in the name of vengeance.

By all rights, Boris, cold and calculating Boris, who never hesitated to shoot when they'd faced enemy troops, should have ended Gene's life back on that impromptu battleground. But his old army buddy chickened out and instead of killing the moose for his lack of nerve, Gene let his emotional demons send him fleeing. He fled for the ice plains, alive, for now.

I might still die yet.

In siding with Boris to save Jan so Gene could have his chance at a fight, he had done the unforgivable. He'd intentionally acted against *his* plan. It wasn't enough that Gene walked out without a word of where he was going, no longer interested in the plot to overthrow Reid and take over the clan at Kodiak Point. Gene had actively fought against *his* army.

That would not go over well at all if the one who'd dragged him from the desert ever found out. And *he* would. *He* always did.

Gene feared few people. He could count them on one hand; the devil when he came to collect his due, his mother, who would have skinned him alive for what he'd done, and *him*.

If the devil was the world's scariest demon, then *he* was the devil's brother. An enemy like no other. While Gene knew what to expect, the others didn't. They might have glimpsed but they certainly had never encountered someone with a core of evil so great, so encompassing, it was a wonder the very foliage didn't wilt under *his* feet.

If Gene ever encountered *him* again, he had no doubt he'd die. Probably painfully, unlike the merciful and quick death Boris could have given him.

Stupid, rotten jerk.

Forgiveness. As if. Just for that, Gene would return, bigger and badder than ever. Eventually. Maybe. But not right yet. First, he needed some time to himself, a moment to regroup and plan.

And he knew just the place to do that. A place where a polar bear could frolic in the cold ocean waves. Sunbathe on sea ice. Catch the freshest fish.

Avoid a pesky—yet cute—little human intent on tagging him and studying his habits for a research piece.

So much for his vacation plans. How was he supposed to plot revenge when he couldn't shake the persistent woman with her camera and inquisitive mind, charting his every move? She was a shifter's worse nightmare and a man's wet dream.

I swear, if she doesn't leave me alone, I'll eat her. And he didn't mean for dinner.

The End of this story.
Next in the series, Polar Bared.

Author's Note: I hope you enjoyed this story. If you did, I'd love it if you took a moment and left a review. To know when my next story will be available, please join my mailing list or for a full list of my books (many of them featuring shifters) visit my website, EveLanglais.com
Thank you for reading. ~ *Eve*